**ALL FOOLS' DAY**

With a rapid movement, the priest lifted his revolver and hit Mumbles with it just below the base of the skull. Mumbles fell without uttering a sound.

'Now,' said Father Jack, turning to Smiler and studying his partial nudity, 'you appear to have been surprised *in flagrante delicto*. Have you any observations to make?'

'Go stuff yourself,' retorted Smiler bravely.

Father Jack sighed. '*Ego te absolvo*, my son.' He shot Smiler neatly through the forehead.

Just another dead boy. A late and indirect casualty of ten years of Omega radiation.

**Also by the same author, and available in Coronet Books:**

Jupiter Laughs
Transit
The Venom Of Argus
The War Games Of Zelos
Death Worms Of Kratos
The Rings Of Tantalus
The Overman Culture
A Far Sunset
Seed Of Light
The Tenth Planet
Seahorse In The Sky
Kronk

# All Fools' Day

---

## Edmund Cooper

CORONET BOOKS
Hodder and Stoughton

First published in Great Britain 1966
by Hodder and Stoughton Limited

*Coronet edition 1967*
*Second impression 1973*
*Third impression 1977*
*Fourth impression 1981*

---



Printed and bound in Great Britain for
Hodder and Stoughton Paperbacks, a
division of Hodder and Stoughton Ltd.,
Mill Road, Dunton Green, Sevenoaks, Kent
(Editorial Office: 47 Bedford Square,
London WC1 3DP) by
Hunt Barnard Printing Ltd.,
Aylesbury, Bucks.

ISBN 0 340 02860 2

Recently, a new and particularly bizarre possibility shows signs of emerging from scientific literature in diverse fields of activity—is there even a remote chance that man's mind could be affected by changing conditions in space?

There are many beginnings to this story, but no explanation and no foreseeable future . . .

The latest thread appeared on November 16th, 1963, in the scientific journal *Nature*, where an account was given by Professors H. Friedman, R.O. Becker and C. H. Bachman, of New York, of their attempts to find some factors correlating with suicides and admissions to mental hospitals. They investigated 28,642 admissions to eight psychiatric hospitals in New York State between 1957 and 1961 and found a significant correlation with magnetic storms.

SIR BERNARD LOVELL
(*Sunday Times*, London, March 16th, 1964)

Dr. Marcel Poumailloux, representing the French Medical Association, said he had studied 1,500 heart cases in Paris over two years and had found that "coronaries" seemed to increase just after periods of intense solar activity.

By checking heart attack rate against data supplied by astronomers, he had found what appeared to be a link with "cosmic ray storms".

PETER FAIRLEY
(*Evening Standard*, London, July 21st, 1964)

## AUTHOR'S NOTE

The sun provides the warmth without which life on Earth could not exist. It is the giver and sustainer of life; but if we were not protected from its fierce energies, it could rapidly become the dealer of death. For the sun is a vast atomic furnace with internal temperatures of 13 million degrees centigrade. It consumes itself at the rate of 4 million tons a second, releasing unimaginable torrents of radiation. We are protected from the full force of this energy by the atmosphere and the magnetosphere, where solar particles are trapped in the Van Allen belts.

The slightest variation in the sun's release of energy or in the power of the magnetosphere to protect us from dangerous radiation could produce incalculable results. *All Fool's Day* is science fiction and is concerned with the possible effects of such a variation. The story opens in 1971; but it might just as well begin in 1981 or, indeed, at any time in the future. For mankind can never be immune from a touch of the sun.

# ONE

July 7th, 1971. Two-thirty a.m. The air warm, clear patches of sky loaded with stars, and the Thames rippling quietly through the subdued noises of London like a jet and silver snake.

Two-thirty a.m. A car whispering sweetly, as cars do in the moist hours of darkness. A car, a man and a woman, routed for Chelsea from Kingston. A man and a woman journeying from the good life to the good life. A man with a bellyful of misery and loneliness and some precious dregs of self-respect—driving in top gear to a centrally-heated, sound-proofed limbo with an original Picasso and the latest Scandinavian furniture . . .

Matthew Greville, aged twenty-seven, ex-human being and adman of this city had been drunk and was now sober. As he drove, he glanced occasionally at his wife, Pauline, wondering if such sobriety could be contagious. Evidently not.

Where did sobriety begin and intoxication end? Perhaps it began about eight miles back with a cat. The cat was black, fat, old and—as Pauline had remarked with comfortable assurance—obviously filled with the death-wish. It had come streaking across the road like a wild thing in pursuit of sex, rats or possibly nothing more substantial than visions.

There had been a moment of choice when Greville could have put on the brakes and sent up a hurried prayer to the Cats' God. He had had the time and he wanted to stamp on the brake pedal. The odd thing was that his foot wouldn't move.

The cat passed under the car. There was a bump. Finally, Greville managed to move his foot. The car screeched reproachfully to a stop.

"What, may I ask, is this in aid of?" said Pauline gently.

"I hit a cat."

"So?"

"So I'd better see whether the poor wretch is dead."

"There are too many cats," remarked Pauline. "Does it matter? I'm rather tired."

"There are too many cats," agreed Greville, "but oddly it matters, and I'm tired, too."

"Darling, don't be lugubrious. It was such a nice party. I'm not in the mood for suicidal cats."

Greville was suddenly disgusted—with himself. "I won't be a minute." He got out of the car and slammed the door.

He found the cat about thirty yards back. It was not dead. It had rolled into the gutter and its back was horribly twisted, but there was no sign of blood.

"Die, please die," murmured Greville. Ashamed, he knelt down and stroked the cat's head. It shuddered a little, then nuzzled him, leaving blood upon his hands. It seemed pathetically grateful for his attention.

"Pussy, please, *please* die," he coaxed.

But the cat clung obstinately to life. Then the pain came, bringing with it thin, bubbling screams.

Greville could stand it no longer. He eased his hand under the animal and suddenly lifted it up. There was a final cry of anguish before the edge of his other hand came down with all the strength he could muster. The force of the blow took the cat from his grasp and returned it heavily to the gutter. But its neck was broken, and after one or two twitches there was only stillness.

He stood there shaking for a few moments. Then he went back to the car.

"I presume you found the beast?" said Pauline coldly.

"It was rather badly messed up. I—I had to kill it."

"Did you, indeed! Then, for goodness' sake don't touch me until you've had a bath ... You have to make a production of every damn thing, don't you, darling?"

He said nothing. He settled himself in the driver's seat and turned on the ignition. After a few minutes he was surprised to notice that he was dawdling along at less than forty miles an hour. But perhaps that was because he was already becoming sober.

Or drowning ...

People are traditionally expected to review their lives when drowning. Therefore, concluded Greville, he was drowning. For the memories were coming thick and fast.

Life (was it really life?) began with Pauline. Five years

ago when one of her stiletto heels got stuck in a metal grating in the Strand. It was an evening in late autumn. He rescued the shoe and made so bold as to buy her some hot and deliciously aromatic chestnuts. They talked. He took her home to a surprisingly comfortable three-girl flat in Notting Hill Gate.

There were other meetings. Regular meetings. She was in advertising and ambitious. He was in an oil company and frustrated. They both thought he had talent. Greville thought he could write poetry and was even prepared to accept the prostitution of novels. Pauline thought he could write copy. High-class copy for high-class ads. Temptation for Top People.

Before he knew what had happened, he had a job at twice the salary and half the work. The great and glorious mantle of the adman had wrapped itself comfortably round his shoulders. He still thought it was because he had talent. He did not discover until much later—after they were married—that it was because Pauline also had talent.

Hers was more formidable. It consisted of an easy manner with executives and clients, an affinity for bedrooms, a body that seemed somehow to carry a written guarantee, and a mind like a digital computer.

Greville climbed fast. And the funny thing was that for two years he didn't know who was holding the ladder.

He discovered it in the most conventional of ways—quite by accident when he returned from a Paris conference one night too soon. By that time, Greville and Pauline had a flat in a new block in Holland Park. It was a nice flat, high up, with views over London and two bedrooms.

Greville had arrived at London Airport just after eleven o'clock. He let himself quietly into the flat just before midnight. He had made the stealthy approach in case Pauline was asleep. There were the remains of drinks in the living-room—two glasses—and a blue haze of cigarette smoke.

At first he was glad that Pauline had had company. He thought he must have just missed the visitor. Then Pauline's voice coming muffled from the bedroom—excited and inarticulate—told him that he had not quite missed the visitor. Logically enough, the second voice belonged to the man who had given him the opportunity of rubbing shoulders with the great at the European Project conference in Paris.

Indecision. Masochism. Cowardice.

Greville listened to the sounds in the bedroom. He sentenced himself to listen, taking a terrible satisfaction in his own humiliation. Then, when all was quiet, he simply went away.

He found himself a hotel at Marble Arch, spent the rest of the night drinking duty-free cognac, and returned to Pauline at the appointed time. He never told her about it, and he never again returned from a trip unexpectedly. But thereafter he kept the score. He let her see that he was keeping the score just so that she would not get too careless. She never did.

Accounts came Greville's way, all kinds of accounts from steel to lingerie. So did private commissions. And consultancies.

No longer an ordinary account executive—let other people do the work—he concerned himself with policy and strategy. And the money kept on rolling.

Holland Park, Portman Square, Victoria, and now eighteen thousand pounds-worth of status residence in Chelsea. A Picasso and Scandinavian furniture. Success. Success. Success . . .

"Darling," said Pauline bisecting his reverie with her number one conciliatory voice. "I was talking to Wally Heffert while you were laying it on for the Evans girl."

"That must have been nice for you."

"Oh, well, he's quite a cheery old stick."

Dull, divorced and loaded, thought Greville. Wally Heffert, king of Heffert, McCall and Co. Lord High Custodian of three frozen foods, a dozen cigarette brands, Trans-Orient Air Lines and the Junior Joy contraceptive pill. Therefore by definition a "cheery old stick". Pauline's natural prey.

"He thinks a lot of your work," she went on. "He'd like to talk to you about a retainer. Heffert McCall are getting more than they can handle . . . It would be quite a big slice, I imagine."

"How long have you been sleeping with him?" asked Greville conversationally, keeping his eyes on the road.

"Please don't be immature, darling. That stupid cat must have upset you."

For Pauline, "immature" was a multi-purpose word. It could equal obscene, petulant, idealistic, depraved, old-fashioned, naïve or honest—depending upon the occasion and the context.

In the present instance, it clearly equalled obscene plus petulant.

Greville turned the car towards Chelsea Bridge. The speedometer needle crept high once more. He did not know it, but he had just made a decision.

He turned to Pauline. "Do you know, darling, I think I'm actually sober."

Suddenly, she sensed that something was wrong—badly wrong.

"What the hell are you talking about, Matthew?"

Chelsea Bridge was before them. A slightly arched ribbon of road. There was nothing else on the road. There was nothing but the sky and the river.

"Being alive, that's all. My God, it hurts!"

Sixty-five, seventy, seventy-five, eighty ...

"Stop the car! Do you hear? Stop the car!"

He turned and smiled at her. There was affection in his voice. Even compassion. Because at last he felt that he could afford to forgive.

"Dear Pauline," he said. "It's no good only one of us being sober. Why don't we stop the world?"

They both tore at the wheel. The car skipped crazily against the steelwork of the bridge. Then it somersaulted twice and landed on its side.

Greville, still alive, found that he was lying almost on top of Pauline. Her eyes were open, reminding him of the cat. But this time there was no problem ... She still looked beautiful; and, for a moment, he was sure he could smell roasting chestnuts ...

Then he tried to move. And the tears in his eyes mingled with his own blood.

A few minutes later, another car began to cross Chelsea Bridge. And a little after that an ambulance and a police car came.

## TWO

UNTIL early July the summer had been a typically English summer—that is to say, despite manned weather satellites and computer-based long-range forecasts, it had remained as unpredictable as ever, confounding scientists, prophets, farmers and tourists alike. One day the sky would be clear and the sun hot; and the next day torrential downpours would reduce the temperature to a level plainly indicating warmer underwear.

But by the middle of July it began to look as if the summer might possibly settle down into one of those vintage seasons that everybody remembers from childhood, though nobody can actually pin down the year. Each day, after early mists, the sky became abnormally clear. The heat was not too intense, and light breezes made life pleasant enough for those who still had to go to work.

July passed, August came—and still the good weather persisted. It was not confined to the British Isles or even to Europe. Most of the countries in the Northern Hemisphere basked in what was truly a golden season. Later, it would be the turn of the Southern Hemisphere to enjoy the fantastic run of weather. But no one was yet to know that, for the next ten years throughout the world, summertime was going to break all known records.

Matthew Greville, however, was among the minority who remained quite uninterested in the weather; and, in fact, he was largely unaffected by it during the next three years. The crash that killed Pauline merely dealt him multiple head injuries. He remained in hospital until September, while the surgeons made a thoroughly efficient job of saving the sight of his left eye and restoring muscular control of the left side of his body. At the same time, the psychiatrists were busy persuading him that life could still be worth living. As it turned out, their task was rather more difficult than that of the surgeons. But eventually they at least got him to a state in which he was fit to plead.

The police had taken considerable interest in the "accident", since there had been no other cars on the bridge at the time. They measured the tyre marks, interviewed people who had been at the party in Kingston—including one Walter Heffert of Heffert, McCall and Co.—and took statements from Greville himself. The result of all this activity crystallised into two charges. Manslaughter and Dangerous Driving. Greville collected sentences totalling three years, which he found monstrously unjust. He would have preferred the death penalty.

It was not until the first week in October, about the time that Greville was being transferred to one of the better-class English prisons for better-class English criminals, that the long and utterly glorious summer came to its end. Though there had been enough nocturnal rainfall and light daytime showers to keep the crops healthy, there had been ten weeks of virtually uninterrupted sunshine. It was followed by a month of intermittent rain—and floods.

Some curious facts began to emerge about the summer. There had been roughly three times the average amount of sunshine for the period. There had also been about five times the average number of suicides. This was spectacular enough to make the front pages of most of the newspapers. Prominence was also given to the discovery that new sun-spots had appeared and had been emitting a new type of radiation. The facts that the radiation possessed properties hitherto unknown to science and that the surplus suicides exhibited symptoms hitherto unknown to psychiatry gave rise to considerable speculation.

The name given to the waves (or were they particles?) emitted from the sun-spots was Omega radiation—chiefly because the scientists were baffled and because every fruitful investigation seemed destined to be a long-term project. The name eventually given to the fivefold increase in self-destruction (by a journalist who drowned himself a few weeks later) was the Radiant Suicide.

It was the popular press that had first suggested a "statistical relationship" between Omega radiation and what everyone now called the Radiant Suicide. The idea triggered off a chain reaction among scientists, religious leaders, psychologists and plain cranks.

One so-called scientist "borrowed" two groups of children from a well-meaning if mentally retarded headmaster with a proper respect for Scientific Method. The scientist kept one lot of children in a cellar for long spells while the other lot were compelled to spend most of their time in the open air exposed to sunlight. Not surprisingly, he found that after a day or two of this kind of treatment the open-air group could do sums much faster and more accurately than the cellar group. From this he appeared to conclude (a) that Omega radiation stimulated intellectual activity and could therefore induce nervous exhaustion, and (b) that anybody who wanted to avoid nervous exhaustion and, therefore, suicide would be well advised to live underground. Having the courage of his convictions, he himself took to a subterranean existence—and committed suicide two months later.

The psychologists and psychiatrists were rather more reluctant to link the increase in the suicide rate with Omega radiation—chiefly because radiation was outside their province. They took a more esoteric approach and began to fling about such phrases as "thyroidal displacement", "societal emotional imbalance", "liberation of the collective death-wish", "induced hyper-mysticism" and "cathartic destruction". The Radiant Suicide, apparently, was quite explicable. In a world in which the idea of war was rapidly becoming absurd, it was modern man's neurotic simulation of the consequences of tribal conflict. Eventually the psychologists and psychiatrists produced so many plausible explanations of the Radiant Suicide as to convey the impression that they had almost invented it.

However, for the most part the religious fanatics took a simpler view. It was merely an Awful Warning sent by God. We would have to mend our ways or else . . .

But while the cranks of various persuasions were airing their pet philosophies and producing equally useless panaceas, a few intelligent people were busy collating the facts.

And the facts that emerged were these:

1. Until shortly before the detection of Omega radiation, the suicide rate was approximately normal.

2. The incidence of suicide increased with the incidence of radiation.

3. Cloudy weather tended to slow down the rate of increase perceptibly but not significantly.

4. Though there had been tremendous increases in the suicide rate throughout the world, the increases in the Northern Hemisphere had so far been slightly larger than in the Southern Hemisphere.

5. The types of people affected were those who, under normal conditions, would be considered the least prone to suicidal impulses.

6. Many people who had either failed in their attempts to commit suicide or had been rescued by others reported that, shortly before the urge to self-destruction, they had experienced tremendous sensations of peacefulness and of identification with something greater than self. A common element of their reports was the widespread conviction that death would render the experience absolute or permanent.

7. The intensity of the Omega radiation was still increasing, and many astronomers expressed the view that the new sun-spots could be expected to remain "active" for a considerable period of time.

These were the facts. And they were responsible for sending the sales of sedatives, tranquillisers, alcoholic drinks and Bibles soaring to unprecedented heights.

By the end of 1971, thirty-four thousand people in the United Kingdom had taken their own lives—yet the statistical expectation was only six thousand five hundred. The Home Secretary, woolly-minded as ever, recommended that suicide be treated as a criminal offence once more. It was anti-social, he said, and definitely bad for the country's economy. So a bill was rapidly pushed through Parliament. It came to be briefly immortalised as the "Do Yourself In Deterrent". For one of its provisions was that one-third of the estate of any suicide (after death duty) *could* be claimed in forfeit by the State. Another provision was that attempted suicide *could* be punished by a maximum of ten years' imprisonment. The bill, needless to say, was totally ineffective—but it contributed somewhat to the government being overthrown six months later.

Meanwhile Matthew Greville was adapting himself to

the routines of prison life. It was far more comfortable than he had imagined; and this, in itself, proved a major frustration because he believed that he ought to be made to suffer—not only for Pauline, but for the very uselessness and pointlessness of his life. For all the minor deceits he had ever practised, for all the little vanities he had ever developed, for the talent he had wasted, the ideals he had abandoned, and for every cliché-ridden perverted ethic he had ever subscribed to in admanland. Suicide would appear to have been the perfect answer—perhaps it might have been on July 7th, 1971. But he had spent months trying to analyse his intentions and motives, and he was no wiser. Did he really intend to kill himself on Chelsea Bridge? Or Pauline, or both of them? Or was he only indulging in a melodramatic gesture that got out of control?

If he hadn't killed the cat ... If Pauline hadn't grabbed at the wheel ... If ... If ... If ...

There was no satisfactory solution—not even suicide. For that was now only a sort of luxury. He wanted to be punished, he wanted to be hurt, he wanted to feel again the strange anguish of being alive ...

During his entire stay in prison seven warders and fifty-four prisoners committed suicide. As a penance for existing and a reward for not killing himself, Greville became the self-appointed gravedigger-in-chief.

Throughout the short and fairly dry winter of 1972, the Omega radiation intensified. So did the Radiant Suicide. And the pessimists were already predicting a warm dry summer.

Science and human ingenuity came up with a remarkable number of solutions—none of them satisfactory and some of them dangerous. One of the many new "tranquil stimulants" coming out of the laboratories of the manufacturing chemists in hysterical haste (this particular drug was marketed as Positive Pep) was responsible for more than a hundred thousand miscarriages or premature births, and therefore contributed quite significantly to the increase in the suicide rate. Another one was more effective in preventing suicide—but one of its side effects was to produce delusions of grandeur. A third was equally effective in preventing people from killing themselves: the problem was that it tended to create addiction, and addiction overloaded the heart.

Thousands of "mental hygiene" groups were formed, an organisation called Death-Wish Anonymous sprang into existence, dozens of different sects, disciplines and esoteric societies mushroomed. And religious revival became a major industry.

But, despite everything, by the end of 1972 (again there had been an utterly glorious summer) more than a hundred and twenty thousand people in the United Kingdom alone had taken their own lives. The proportional increase was similar in most other countries.

Meanwile, the Omega radiation—the most elusive and enigmatic form of radiant energy ever discovered—intensified. And while researchers into its nature remained baffled, researchers into its effects came up with more interesting data.

It had been discovered that Omega-proof shields could be devised. All you needed was a wall of lead sixteen feet thick, or a thicker wall of less dense material. But even this was no good unless the people to be shielded by it remained permanently shielded. Anyone prone to what was abbreviated to Radiant-S, or simply R.S., needed only a few minutes exposure to trigger off the reaction. The only variable was the time factor. It could be months before the R.S. impulse manifested itself, or merely a matter of hours.

Another interesting discovery was that all children were "R.S.-proof" until the age of puberty. And, in fact, from puberty until about the age of twenty-five (the presumed end of growth and adolescence) the risk of R.S. was only about half as great as for the rest of the population.

But, most curious of all, was the emerging classification of R.S. types. During the first two years the information gathered from more than a hundred and fifty thousand victims indicated that, in terms of professions and vocations, the most susceptible types were bank clerks, accountants, scientists, executives and managers of all kinds, shopkeepers, typists, dons (but not teachers!), pilots, sea captains, bus drivers, engine drivers, mathematicians, professional gamblers and bookmakers, *minor* politicians, watchmakers and civil servants. Spinsters, or—more accurately—virgins over the age of twenty-five were a very heavy risk: so were bachelors similarly.

The least likely R.S. subjects were creative artists of all kinds, lunatics, political and religious fanatics, actors, dancers and entertainers, cranks, homosexuals, prostitutes, eccentrics, doctors and nurses, teachers, sportsmen, sadists, masochists and pathological animal lovers.

Clearly, it was now a case of, "*Do* send your daughter on the stage, Mrs Worthington." But strategems of this kind were not much good if the person concerned happened to have a repressed flair for, say, mathematics.

1973 came. And went—after another brilliant summer. The final reckoning in Britain was just under half a million R.S. victims. Added to which a secondary reaction was now apparent. The birth rate was falling, for obvious reasons; and the natural death rate was rising, for equally obvious reasons. People were beginning to be afraid to have children and, ironically, they were also indirectly killing themselves with worry. Towards the end of the year Parliament reintroduced conscription—which had been out of favour for more than a decade. However, the need this time was not for soldiers but for burial squads, bus drivers and clerical workers.

In the autumn of 1974, having served his full term after contriving to avoid remission for good conduct by deliberately assaulting a prison officer, Matthew Greville was released from prison. He was given a rail ticket to London and the sum of eighteen pounds nine shillings and sixpence, which he had earned in his capacity as gravedigger.

He had no home to go to, since he had long ago instructed his solicitor to sell the Chelsea residence and all it contained. There had been quite a large mortgage to pay off. Nevertheless, when all assets (including the Picasso) had been realised, the solicitor was able to deposit just over eleven thousand pounds in Greville's account. Greville had promptly disposed of the entire amount to various charities.

When he arrived in London, he hired a taxi and toured the city, savouring its richness and its bustle (for despite the Radiant Suicide London still managed to put on a brave face), noting the changes, the new skyscraper blocks that were still going up—and the new churches that were being built. Then he told the taxi driver to take him to Chelsea Bridge, where he got out, paid off the taxi and began to walk across.

The dents were still there in the steelwork. He had to look carefully for them, but they were still there. They had been painted over, and two or three badly twisted metal sections had been renewed, but the hidden hieroglyphs still proclaimed the final result of life with Pauline—and, perhaps, the result also of an encounter with an unknown cat.

He stared for a while at the message that none but he could decipher. The sky was misty blue, and the sun covered all of England with the gold and ripening light of autumn. It was a perfect day. But the weather was entirely lost upon Greville. After reliving yet again the strange drive from Kingston (only three years ago, but in another kind of time) he headed for the nearest bar and proceeded to get drunk.

He stayed drunk for three days, at the end of which time he woke up early in the morning in Hyde Park—shaking with the effects of drink and nervous tension, and remembering little of what had passed since his visit to the bridge.

He pulled himself together and inquired the way to the nearest army recruitment centre. He had to wait an hour for it to open. The military gentlemen in charge were not filled with joy at the prospect of enlisting a jailbird and an obvious tramp. However, after some deliberation they magnanimously allowed him to volunteer for the Emergency Burial Corps. He was pathetically grateful. This was the kind of work he wanted—just as in prison. It was a public service.

By the end of 1974, one million two hundred thousand British subjects had committed suicide.

The first large holes in the fabric of society were becoming apparent. Transport was strained to breakdown point. It began to take as long as a week for a letter to get from London to the cities of the Industrial North. Rationing of food and fuel was reintroduced. The gas supplies were still unaffected; but shortage of coal and fuel oil and irregular deliveries was responsible for domestic electricity only being available between fixed hours. A bill for the Direction of Labour was quickly pushed through the House. It provided powers by which every male between eighteen and sixty-five could be re-directed to more vital work at a week's notice. The Direction bill helped a little—that is to say, it delayed the inevitable and ultimate breakdown—but its main function seemed to be to enable the government, and the society it represented, to make a fairly orderly withdrawal . . . A withdrawal from the more complex functions of a civilised community . . .

And still the Omega radiation poured invisibly, painlessly and maddeningly from the remote face of the sun. And still the scientists (now heavily depleted) struggled to find some kind of efficient protection or even immunisation. And still the R.S. rate climbed.

In 1975 it passed the three million mark. Matthew Greville, private in the E.B.C., no longer dug graves by hand. He used a mechanical excavator. Then he operated a bulldozer to push the piles of thin plastic coffins into long communal graves.

At the end of 1976, the year's death roll touched ten million. Three separate emergency governments were operating autonomously in the North, the Midlands and the South. Coffins were obsolete. All manufactured materials were needed by the living.

1977. Another glorious summer. The emergency governments had now disintegrated into eleven regional councils. Rail travel was suspended indefinitely except for fuel and food between some major cities. Typhoid fever raged in London; rioting in Edinburgh, York and Birmingham; starvation in South Lancashire and North Cheshire. Stealing, "desertion" and withholding of labour became punishable by death in seven of the eleven regions . . . Total death roll: fifteen and a half million.

Matthew Greville, temporary major in the London Emergency Burial Corps, was captured by slavers from the Midlands. Heavy chains were fastened round his ankles, and together with a group of other "foreign recruits" he was sent down a mine in the Province of Nottingham to hew coal. Like the pit ponies with which they worked and died, the foreign recruits were kept permanently below the surface. The rations sent down to them varied according to the coal they sent up. Needless to say, the mortality rate was high.

1978. The total death roll in what had formerly been known as the United Kingdom was estimated by the statistics section of the Second London Commune to be in the region of eight million.

Towards the end of 1978 Matthew Greville escaped from the mine by feigning death and contriving to accept in silence a routine bayonet thrust. This was the method by which tired inspectors normally contrived to discover such attempts in their examination of the twice weekly burial cart. Greville's wound, three inches deep, surprisingly did not pierce any vital organs. After a period of hiding, during which he endured mild fever and some starvation, he escaped from the Province of Nottingham and was almost immediately recruited by the Leicester City Volunteer Force as an unskilled farm labourer. The work was considerably easier than mining; but the food was not so good in quantity or quality. He lost weight, his hair began to turn grey, then white. But he remained alive and remarkably healthy.

In 1979 the Second London Commune disintegrated. So did practically all similar organisations throughout the British Isles, Europe and the entire world. Matthew Greville, one of the hundred and fifty thousand people still occupying the off-shore islands once literally described as Great Britain, was a free man again—living on a hand-to-mouth basis.

The Radiant Suicide—less selective as a result of the three preceding years of very intense Omega radiation—had taken the high and the low, the intelligent and the intellectually subnormal, the strong and the weak, the old and the young. In the end, all it had left as custodians of the future of mankind were the emotionally disturbed—the cranks, the misfits, the fanatics, the obsessionals, the geniuses, the idiots, the harmless eccentrics, the homicidal maniacs, the saints and sinners extraordinary who had never found peace or happiness or understanding in an ordinary world.

Now there was no longer an ordinary world. The ordinary, the average, the normal—as a way of existence, as a standard of behaviour—was obsolete. There was no accepted ethic left—apart from personal survival

—to which anyone could be expected to conform. All that remained was . . . transnormal . . .

In 1980, the Omega radiation became very slightly less intense. But there were no scientists left to measure its intensity, or even to verify that the sun-spots producing it were still active.

1980 was chaos.

## THREE

July 7th, 1981 (perhaps). Two-thirty a.m.—Greville mean time. For now that the world was dying, now that there were no more calendars, newspapers, or work days, time was wonderfully subjective. You could declare every day to be Sunday, thought Greville, and every night to be New Year's Eve . . . He was drunk, and he knew he was drunk, and he didn't care a damn . . .

Besides, there was an anniversary to celebrate. The liberation of Matthew Greville, sometime adman of this city. No, a double anniversary! For one must not forget the quietus of Pauline.

Dear, dead Pauline. Likewise a prostitute, but more honest. Likewise a fellow-traveller to eternity. But some bastard had made a reservation for her on the doomsday express.

Who was that bastard?

Answer: Matthew Greville, the poet of the four-colour ad., the ex-extraordinary crap-shitting conman of the stockbroker belt. The Shakespeare of the glossy mag., the Goethe of the *Sunday Times* colour section, the da Vinci of *Woman's Own.*

But where now were the *Sunday Times* and *Woman's Own* and the glory that was *House and Garden*?

All gone into the dark . . .

O dark, dark, dark, amid the blaze of noon . . .

The air was warm, and the sky was a bowl of darkness leaking with a thousand stars, and the Thames still rippled like a fat serpent through the steel and concrete bones of London.

Matthew Greville was sitting in a station wagon on

Chelsea Bridge. The car's bumper was just touching the metalwork where another car had struck it ten years before at something like eighty miles an hour. For a couple of hours now he had been indulging in the society of ghosts—and in brandy, *Salignac* '71, a very fine year . . .

"Did I ever love you, Pauline?" he demanded loudly. "Did I ever give-all-ask-nothing flaming well love you?"

The silence was an answer, accurate and immediate.

"I lusted, my dear," he went on. "I lusted, you lusted, he, she and it lusted . . . Ashes to ashes and lust to lust—the basic philosophy of a world where we needed under-arm deodorants, breath-sweeteners, gin and rubber goods before we could sweat together in fashionable democratic joy."

He hiccupped. "Know what I've been doing since I gave you the final orgasm, darling?" He lifted the bottle of brandy, tried to see how much it still contained by the dashboard light, then took another swig. "Promise not to laugh, and I'll tell you."

The silence was not a laughing silence. The ghost was definitely sober and not at all like the living, fleshly ghost of Pauline.

"I'll tell you," he echoed, finishing off the *Salignac* and flinging the bottle through the open car window. "I've been digging graves—by special appointment . . . You know what I was like, darling. I always had to be best. And, by God, I turned out to be the best bloody gravedigger in history. Immortality at last . . . And do you know how I became the biggest little gravedigger of them all? I'll tell you. I buried mankind, that's how. I buried mankind." His voice broke. "And I want you to know, you poor dead little bitch, that killing you hurt me more than cutting coal, pulling ploughs or shoving a million bodies into the wretched earth . . . That's how much you mean to me, Pauline, because you were the one that stopped me from living. And, goddammit, as if that wasn't enough, you even stopped me from dying . . . Bitch . . . Bitch . . . Dear, lovely bitch!"

Tears were rolling down his face. But Greville did not know that he was crying. For the *Salignac* and the darkness and the memories were too much. He had already fallen asleep. Somewhere, a dog howled; and the sound caused his hand to tighten on the shot-gun that still rested across his knees. The dog howled again and was answered by a chorus of howls. Greville stirred uneasily and groaned, but he did not open his eyes. In the London of 1981 there were not many people who would have dared—drunk or sober—to go to sleep in a car with the window open.

The passing of normal man and the emergence of transnormal man represented either a grotesque end of human development or a new and grotesque beginning. Nobody knew which. The normals, along with their normal processes of evaluation were extinct; and the transnormals didn't seem to care about ends or beginnings—unless they were personal ends and personal beginnings.

All the cities had stopped—like run-down clocks or mechanical toys or deserted hives. Deserted? No, not entirely deserted. For there were the transnormals—so few haunting the great urban graveyards of so many. Like children wandering round an empty mansion ...

But the transnormals were not entirely alone, for when normal man passed into history his very passing created an imbalance in the animal ecology of the planet. The death of three thousand million human beings left not only a great silence but also—as it were —a partial vacuum among living things. And the vacuum was beginning to be filled.

In the cities the wild dogs now roamed—dogs who had survived starvation, disease, cannibalism. Dogs whose wits had been sharpened by hunger, whose civilised conditioning had evaporated almost instantly with the knowledge that man no longer existed as a dog's best friend.

The fancy dogs, the lap dogs, the soft dogs and all the carefully bred triumphs of canine splendour had disappeared. They were the first to die—the poodles, the pekes, the dachshunds, the Yorkshire toys. They were just not tough enough to compete. So they starved or died of grief—or were eaten by the rest.

The sturdy and quick-witted mongrels, the big dogs, the Alsatians, the Great Danes, the boxers, the bulldogs—they survived. They survived to challenge each other. Some of them lived and hunted alone. Some of them hunted and died alone. Many of them learned to trade individualism for the security of the pack. The leaders of the pack maintained the pack law. The only reward was food: the only punishment was death.

It was the same with cats. Except that cats found it harder to shed their individualism. Many of them continued to hunt alone. A few of them formed small groups. They were greatly outnumbered by the dogs, but they were also more ferocious, more unpredictable.

The most numerous of all were the rats. With the withdrawal of normal man, their numbers increased phenomenally. They tended not to hunt in groups or in packs but in swarms. And a swarm of rats was enough to make dogs turn and cats retreat ingloriously to a spitting-point of safety.

The law of the city-jungle was almost a closed circle. Almost but not quite. For the dogs hunted cats, rats and—reluctantly—each other; the cats hunted dogs, rats and—less reluctantly—each other; the rats hunted dogs, cats and—most happily—each other. But all of them hunted man. Especially at night-time when, instinctively, the animals knew they had the advantage.

The rats were to be feared most; for, indifferent to their own losses, their swarms would attack anyone or any living thing at any time. A determined man with a shot-gun had a reasonable chance of shooting his way out of an attack by cats or dogs. But if he was cornered by a rat swarm, his best policy was to turn the gun upon himself.

But, surprisingly, groups of transnormals—or even individuals—still continued to live and move about in the cities. Their numbers were being reduced as the numbers of predators increased. But for many transnormals, the cities were the only places they had truly known. The towers of concrete and steel, the silent streets, the vacant windows and smokeless chimneys of a once normal environment still continued to provide an illusion of security. Until the food ran out, until the water supply failed, or until the rats came . . .

In the countryside the change was no less dramatic, but different. Despite the fact that Britain had been a highly industrialised country, four-fifths of the land had still been used for farming—even up till the early 1970s. But by the time the Radiant Suicide had taken its full toll, the English countryside had begun to revert rapidly.

The wind blew fences down, and there was no one to repair them; low-lying fields became flooded, and no one cleared the ditches for drainage. Animals trampled the hedges, winter ice split and buckled the secondary roads; nettles and ferns, convolvulus and wild hops straddled the rough tracks; sturdy young trees began the slow process of converting pasture into woodland; and in the farmhouses, chimney stacks toppled, roofs caved in and ivy groped whisperingly for a hold on dusty window-panes.

Most of the dairy cows—mild and stupid milk-producing machines—were unable to survive without the symbiotic attention of their masters. But bulls everywhere—unless, being chained up, they were condemned to perish miserably—rejoiced and flourised in their newfound freedom. They crashed through the remaining hedges and competed mightily to woo the surviving cows. Presently some of the cows calved down, and their offspring provided the nucleus of a new yet infinitely older strain. A survival strain.

Pigs were well placed in the survival stakes. When they were hungry enough, they would eat anything that was even vaguely edible—from carrion to the bark of trees. They were lean and hungry brutes, vicious and nimble. Some of them became cannibals, learning craftily to squash or stamp their opponents to death and then trample the corpses until they yielded the life-giving sweetness inside.

Hens—and cocks—also learned to survive. Their minds, narrow and dim and semi-mechanical, only vaguely perceived that something was wrong with the world. Many of the survivors provided satisfactory meals for weasels, dogs, foxes, rats, cats, hawks, eagles and even owls. But the cunning ones took to the trees, made secluded nests for themselves, brought forth young more adaptable and survival-conscious than their parents.

Rabbits multiplied with joyous abandon. So did stoats and weasels and foxes. So did otters and coypus.

And so did the red deer of old England. Small herds of them had been kept in parks here and there over the country. They were among the first of the animals to sense the new freedom conferred on them by the activity of sun-spots nearly a hundred million miles away. They exulted in it. The herds became large. They were not afraid of rats or cats, and they could outrun dogs. They began to spread, reclaiming the land that was once their kingdom.

And there were the horses. Not draught horses or racehorses. Now there was a wilder breed—wild as any slaves that ever survived the years of bondage. There were quick horses, heavy horses, killer horses. They thundered across the land that had once been farmland. Their numbers were still small, but they were growing. They, too, were reclaiming a kingdom.

And on the moors, on Exmoor and Dartmoor and in the New Forest the wild ponies ran. There were no more tourists left to tempt them with sugar. There was only the wind and the rain and the sky, and the rolling pattern of seasons. For normal man, the self-appointed master of all living things, was obsolete. And most of the remaining members of the human race were—for the first time, and in their own way—running wild ...

Greville awoke with a start.

It was the sound of dogs that woke him. The sound of dogs with a quarry in view. The sound of dogs and the sound of rifle or pistol shots.

The grey pre-dawn light was rolling softly up the Thames. Shapes were vague and unfamiliar. The air was still, and there was nothing to suggest that London was not a dead city—nothing except gun shots and the sound of dogs.

Greville yawned and stirred. There was an ache in his back, an ache in his legs, an ache in his head. His tongue felt like the pitted surface of a dirt road. He yawned, cleared his throat, peered through the car window, then looked at his hands. They were fairly steady. He was surprised.

The barking of the dogs came nearer. And now there was another sound. The muted put-put-put of a two-stroke engine.

Greville was curious. Dogs hunting somebody on a

bike or scooter at dawn. Somebody, evidently, had quite a taste for living dangerously.

He checked that the shot-gun was loaded—both barrels—then got out of the car. He sniffed the clean air appreciatively, and listened.

The two-stroke was getting much nearer. Somebody on the South Bank seemed to be heading for Chelsea Bridge—somebody and a retinue of dogs.

He looked along the bridge, but the light was still poor enough to shroud the other end of it in a dark grey obscurity. He breathed deeply and stood there with the shot-gun cradled in his arms. The aches were fading. He was beginning to feel reasonably human.

Suddenly there was a muffled thud, a doggy howl of anguish followed by a barking chorus of triumph. The put-put-put of the two-stroke stopped. It was followed by two shots in rapid succession.

There was movement at the other end of the bridge. Greville could see a figure running towards him. Behind the figure there was a tide of low moving shapes. Hungry and relentless shadows on four legs.

The figure turned and fired once more into the dark carnivorous tide. The fugitive managed to gain a few yards while some of the dogs turned upon their wounded comrade and the others were momentarily checked by renewed fear of the gun. But hunger was greater than fear. The fugitive wasn't going to make it.

The running figure evidently realised that escape was now impossible, for he or she had begun to head from the centre of the bridge to its side. Death by drowning was certainly preferable to death by dogs.

It was at that point that Greville ceased being an interested spectator.

"Over here!" he bellowed. "This way!"

Then he, too, began to run.

He was about forty yards from the still indistinct shape of the fugitive. The dogs were nearer, and they were overhauling fast.

"Drop flat!" shouted Greville.

The fugitive didn't seem to hear or understand.

"Drop flat!" he roared again, brandishing his shot-gun.

This time the command was obeyed.

The figure fell in a sprawling, rolling, untidy heap.

The leaders of the pack were less than a dozen yards from it when Greville let them have the first barrel. One dog collapsed, screaming and writhing, another yelped and turned tail. Three dogs fastened upon their fallen companion.

With a mighty shout, Greville ran towards them. Altogether there were about twenty dogs on the bridge. Their advance was momentarily checked while they considered this new factor.

Greville, still running, was about ten yards from the figure on the ground. He stopped, fired the second barrel at the dogs, broke open his shot-gun, felt in his pocket for two fresh shells and simultaneously shouted: "Crawl here and get behind me, damn you!"

He didn't even look at the person who silently obeyed his command. His attention was taken entirely by the ragged and menacing line of dogs across the bridge.

The light was getting better. They gazed at him malevolently. They knew the power of the thing in his hand, and knew also that its power was not infinite. They snarled and slavered and got ready for the final charge.

He fired again at a dog that seemed to be one of the leaders. Then he swung his gun round and brought down an Alsatian that was trying to outflank him. He knew that he would not get another chance to reload and with a wild and savage cry, he did the impossible, the totally unexpected. He charged the remaining dogs, swinging his shot-gun like a club.

This, itself, was totally outside the experience of the pack. They had seen many humans running—but always away, never towards. They were confounded. And their inability to appreciate Greville's act as an act of desperation led to their undoing.

For a second or two they froze and a lean mongrel fell with a broken neck beneath the butt of Greville's gun. He gave another terrible cry, raised the gun again and brought down a terrier leaping for his stomach. There was a frightful hanging moment of uncertainty, then the rest fled.

With trembling fingers, Greville felt in his pocket for two more shells. He loaded, then began to retreat cautiously backwards towards the car. At the far end of the bridge the dogs were gathering themselves for yet another attack. But they had missed their chance. The crisis was passed.

The figure on the bridge—the fugitive that had crawled behind him like a frightened child—was now hobbling towards the car. Greville glanced at it in amazement.

On the bridge where, just ten years before, he had accidentally(?) killed a woman, he had now accidentally(?) saved one.

He began to laugh. The irony seemed to be of a quality to justify laughter . . .

## FOUR

THE girl's name was Liz. Elizabeth Hopper, age twenty-two, nationality—transnormal. She had escaped on a motor-scooter, she said, from a kind of brothel/hospital /fort in Richmond and she had wildly optimistic hopes of finding her twin sister, recently "liberated" from the same brothel/hospital/fort by a bunch of pirates whose accents had proclaimed their Northern origin. Liz and Jane Hopper, it seemed, were more than just twins: they were super-twins. The degree of empathy or *einfühlung* that existed between them might have provided any normal psychologist of the abnormal with five years of study and a reputation-making monograph on empathetic modes of communication and experience between complemental psychic patterns.

All of this Greville learned in the first ten minutes. All of this and a great deal more.

He had got back to the car to find that the girl had arranged herself comfortably on the passenger seat. Her left leg was troubling her. Evidently she had hurt it when, after running down a particularly enterprising dog, the impact of the collision had thrown her off the scooter.

Greville slammed the door and started the engine. The dogs at the other end of Chelsea Bridge had remembered that breakfast was still in the vicinity. Their numbers had increased—doubtless the commotion had served to recruit all available forces within a radius of a quarter of a mile on the South Bank. They began to pour across the bridge in a solid, bloodthirsty phalanx.

Greville slipped the car into second gear, kept the clutch pedal depressed, and let the engine idle. He waited until the dogs were about twenty yards away. Then his foot came down on the accelerator pedal and the car shot forward with a sharp jerk. He kept the accelerator pedal flat and drove straight at the dogs. They tried to scatter, but they were packed too close together.

His impact speed was about thirty miles an hour. He stayed in second gear, ploughing a bumpy lurching path right through the pack of dogs. The barking, the howls of pain and frustration rose high enough to drown the noise of the engine.

He carried right on to the end of the bridge. Then he did a quick U-turn and came back again. The crushed bodies of half a dozen dogs lay in the roadway. The rest were utterly confused. Some of them tore at their mangled comrades, but most of them stood on the bridge, barking as if the sheer volume of noise would resolve their bewilderment.

Greville drove the station wagon murderously and mercilessly at them. His second pass scored four more victims. At the North Bank he did another U-turn and came thundering back. But the surviving dogs had lost all stomach for the fight. They fled howling. Later, no doubt, they would return to devour the corpses of the fallen. But for the time being breakfast was less important than survival.

Greville turned once more and took the car back to the North Bank, away from the horrible sound of the dogs that had not been killed outright.

He switched off the engine and turned to examine his companion. "Well, that's that," he said calmly. "Let's have a cigarette."

"No, thanks. I don't smoke." Her voice was pleasant. She seemed remarkably self-possessed for one who had so recently avoided a terrible kind of death.

"I'm delighted to hear it. Cigarettes aren't going to

last much longer. One of the most significant tragedies resulting from depopulation. He inspected her without any effort to disguise the fact that he was doing so.

She was wearing a short sheepskin jacket, a faded blue shirt and a pair of men's trousers tucked into calf-length boots. Her hair was short, black and untidy. Her face was pale and bruised. She had the body of a woman and the oddly innocent face of a child. Her eyes were blue and unafraid. She did not seem to mind his inspection at all.

"How is your leg, now?" he asked abruptly.

"Feeling better. It got rather a nasty knock when I came off the scooter. I think it will be all right for walking . . . Would you like me to go, now?"

"Don't be stupid. You'd be dog-meat before you'd done a couple of hundred yards. Where's your gun?"

"I lost it on the bridge."

Greville let out an exasperated sigh. "You're not very interested in surviving, are you?"

She smiled. "I was so busy trying to survive when I saw you that I just forgot all about the gun. Anyway, it was empty."

"Didn't you have any spare ammunition?"

"No."

"Jesus! You're a case, you are. What the hell were you trying to do?"

Then she told him.

He did not find her story hard to believe. In a fantastic world, the fantastic had become merely ordinary.

"So you were setting off with a toy pistol and a motor-scooter to scour the length and breadth of England for sister Jane," he remarked drily when she had finished. "What made you think you were going to live long enough even to get clear of London?"

"I didn't really know what things were going to be like," she confessed. "I haven't been out a great deal in the last two years. They kept us pretty busy, you know."

"Who did?"

"The Richmond Lot."

The Richmond Lot, it transpired, were a group of nearly a hundred men who shared some fifteen to twenty women and were attempting to organise themselves into a tribal group. Their chief was a Canadian ex-wrestler who called himself Johnny Blue Fur—a great hulk of a man whose intelligence-to-weight ratio was possibly an improvement on that of the dinosaur, but not a startling one.

However, surprisingly enough, the Eskimo and French Canadian ancestry of Johnny Blue Fur had produced a mountainous human being who was not only a kindly person but one with a sense of justice. Also, not being in the slightest interested in women, he could remain—as it were—above party conflict.

The reign of Johnny Blue Fur seemed destined to be quite a long and remarkably peaceful one—until the arrival of about thirty well-armed men from the north. They came in a couple of ancient army trucks, and they did not come as enemies but simply as a band of men "on the scrounge". After having made it clear that there was nothing to be scrounged in Richmond—a fact which he gently underlined by assembling his own scroungers, complete with rifles, sub-machine guns and pistols—Johnny Blue Fur hospitably invited them to stay the night at The House.

The House was one of those large, rambling Victorian mansions that had been built on the banks of the Thames for the greater glory of nineteenth-century industrialists. Now, at the beginning of the last two decades of the twentieth century it had been transformed into a combined brothel, hospital, headquarters, chief's residence and storehouse for the Richmond Lot.

Johnny Blue Fur was simple enough, despite the anxious warnings of his lieutenants, to believe that the visitors would not abuse his hospitality—particularly in view of his numerical superiority in arms and men. But the Northerners (who were rather vague about their origin and would say no more than that they had "a little place in Lancashire") were resolute, avaricious and very well organised. Far better organised than the Richmond Lot.

They were tough, they were short of weapons and women, and they had no intention of going away empty-handed.

Johnny Blue Fur laid on a lavish party for their benefit. The wine was passed around freely, and so were the women—among them Liz and Jane who, being twins, seemed to be especially favoured. The party did not break up until about a couple of hours before dawn.

An hour later, when most of the Richmond Lot were deep in their boozy slumbers and even The House guard was dozing, the Northerners came very much to life. Evidently they had only appeared to drink a lot, or else their capacity was quite remarkable.

There was very little shooting. In the dark it was difficult to tell friend from enemy, and there was neither the time nor the opportunity to light oil lamps.

For about five minutes sheer pandemonium existed. Johnny Blue Fur distinguished himself by throwing three men (one of them his own) through a second-storey window before he was felled by a rifle butt. And one of the guards in the grounds managed to cut down four of the raiders with a burst from his sub-machine gun as they ran to their trucks. Then he himself was shot.

But the Northerners managed to get away with six of the women (some of whom were probably too drunk or too exhausted to care), eight rifles and about two hundred rounds of ammunition. Liz might also have been taken as well as Jane, for she had had to spend what was left of the night with one of the visitors. But when he snatched her up, she began to scream and struggle. Then he panicked and tried to strangle her into submission, but somehow she managed to kick him in the stomach; and while he was recovering from that, she crawled away and was lost in the darkness and confusion.

Apparently she and Jane had been almost literally inseparable. They had been "requisitioned" by the Richmond Lot—and saved from probable death by starvation or transnormal causes—in the summer of 1979. Prostitution, defined grandly by Johnny Blue Fur as free love, turned out not to be quite as repulsive as either of them had feared. At least they had enough food and were relatively safe. And when things could be shared, they did not seem quite so bad. But with Jane's forced departure—which had taken place several days ago—a curious feeling of deadness came over Liz. It was as if she had been given a tremendous dosage of local anaesthetic in mind and body. Nothing mattered any more. Nothing, that is, except finding Jane somehow and finding a way of being together again. She decided to escape from the Richmond Lot at the first opportunity.

Greville had listened to the rest of her recital for the most part in silence. It did not surprise him. There was very little that could surprise him these days.

When she had finished, he said: "So now you are my problem."

"Not if you don't want me to be," said Liz simply.

"I saved your life, didn't I?"

"Yes."

"Then it seems reasonable for me to have a controlling interest in it."

"Have you got a woman?" she asked bluntly.

"No."

"Do you want one?"

"I don't know. I hadn't thought about it."

"Well, you'd better think about it," she said practically. "But if you just want a good screw, make up your mind and let's get it over with. Then we can go our own ways."

Her calmness annoyed him. Once more Greville inspected her critically—this time as if he was mentally undressing her. She remained unembarrassed.

"I never make love before noon," he remarked humourlessly.

"Who said anything about love?" she retorted. "It's something people like me have to do to stay alive."

Greville refused to let himself show any pity, because pity was nothing more than placing a weapon in the hands of an opponent. "I suppose even people like you develop a taste for it."

"Especially people like me," said Liz. "And especially if we get screwed about twice a day for a year or two. We either jump in the river or develop a taste for it." She returned his critical inspection with interest. "Mind you," she added, "there are times when it's repulsive anyway, but I've learned to put up with them."

Greville slapped her. It was not a very hard blow, but surprisingly she began to cry.

Despite the implications of her last remark, he didn't

know why he had slapped her—just as he didn't know why he was now putting his arm round her shoulder and trying to comfort her.

"It wasn't you. It wasn't you," she sobbed. "It was those horrible dogs . . . Oh, hell, I want to be sick."

Greville opened the car door and helped her out. She retched, but very little came up. When she had finished, she began to shiver violently. With the shotgun in his hand and keeping an alert eye for dogs, he made her walk up and down until the shivering stopped.

"Thanks," she said at last. "I seem to be thanking you for everything, don't I?"

"It's a habit you'll grow out of."

"Yes . . . I don't even know your name."

"Call me Greville."

"Is that all of it?"

"It's enough."

Liz sighed. "Well, what are you going to do with me, Greville?"

"I don't know. I shall have to think about it."

"Don't think too long. If you don't want your pound of flesh, I'm going to try and get a bit nearer Jane."

He laughed. "You've got about as much chance of finding Jane, as of finding a needle in the proverbial but now obsolete haystack."

"What's that to you?" demanded Liz wearily. "We're all nut-cases together. Besides, I have a sort of built-in direction-finding apparatus. And, anyway, it doesn't matter how I waste my time, does it?"

"It matters to me," said Greville. And suddenly he was amazed to realise that it did. "It's quite a long time since I talked to anybody," he said, as if that explained everything. "I think I might take you home with me. You might even be useful."

"I'm no good for anything but screwing," said Liz flatly.

"For all I know you might not even be any good at that. Incidentally, while we're on the subject, try to find another word for it."

"Does it offend your modesty?"

"No," he said evenly. "Only my aesthetic sense. Now, if you have got over having the vapours, let's think in terms of breakfast."

# FIVE

Breakfast consisted of very salty ham, coarse home-made bread and bottled beer. They ate it near Cleopatra's Needle, on the Embankment. It was a long time since Liz had been in London, and she wanted to see what time, transnormals, and the reign of cats and dogs had done to it. She was not haunted by ghosts as Greville was, and she was fifteen years younger. Also she had never really known the normal world, for all her growing and most of her exploring had been done during the terrible decade of Omega radiation. So she could not experience the perspective of sadness that Greville experienced, nor could she be aware as he was aware of the immense tragedy in the passing of a great city. If she did not seem to notice the desolation so much it was simply because experience had taught her that this kind of desolation was natural: it was just a part of life.

They ate their meal sitting in the car and watched the sun climb slowly with the bright golden promise of another warm day. The food was part of the rations Greville had brought with him on his obsessional anniversary visit to Chelsea Bridge. There had, of course, been a practical excuse for the long—and hazardous—expedition from his cottage in Norfolk to the great city. He was on the scrounge—for guns, ammunition, shoes, clothing, tools, books, and almost anything.

He had been living in East Anglia for about eighteen months. He had drifted there and found the cottage that he had made into his private lair purely by chance. When the Leicester Volunteer Force disintegrated in 1979—along with practically every other quasi-social organisation in the country—he had almost instinctively made his way south. On his wanderings he had become entangled, and rapidly disentangled, with several small groups of one kind or another. But he had not attached himself or allowed himself to become personally involved for the very simple reason that he knew that most of the groups he had encountered were doomed. Some of them had been no more than amateur brigands, others were small tribes based loosely on the family and recognising only the ties of real or symbolic kinship, yet others were fanatical do-gooders trying with a few dozen hands to resurrect the body and spirit of an entire civilisation. But none of them had staying power because they were either living on the past or trying to rebuild it. They could not understand that, in the broad sense, they were nothing more than grave-robbers—like Egyptian peasants looting from the Valley of the Tombs of Kings.

Greville was disgusted with failure, his own and everyone else's. So he recoiled from membership of a group—any group—and determined to lead a fairly solitary existence. Above all, he needed time to think, time to come to terms with a mad world, time to come to terms with his own private madness.

He had discovered the cottage in Norfolk as he struggled vaguely towards London. It was more than a cottage: it was a citadel, for it stood on an island less than an acre in size in Ambergreave Lake, about twenty miles south of Norwich. There had once been an Ambergreave Manor, a rambling sixteenth-century mansion, that had been burned down in 1976 when the owner poured two gallons of petrol over himself and struck a match. The cottage on the island had originally been built as a folly at a time when such architectural extravagances were popular attractions in the grounds of large English country houses. But a nineteenth-century Lord of Ambergreave, who took a serious and considerably optimistic view of his qualities as a poet, had the folly converted to a retreat where he could live in splendid isolation for weeks at a time while churning out an abundance of sonnets that would surely establish a considerable niche for him in English literary history.

Unfortunately, it did not occur to him that English Literature itself was subject to mortality. Nor could he have possibly entertained the notion that within five years of his death his poems would be forgotten by everyone but the printer to whom he had paid in the course of time more than a thousand guineas for the publication of various slim volumes.

Such, however, proved to be the case. Greville had discovered his effigy in marble above a substantial-looking vault in the churchyard of the village of Ambergreave, which was about three miles away from the remains of the manor house. The grave—and, in fact, the entire churchyard—was rapidly disappearing under a mass of weeds and shrubs. But he had been sufficiently interested in the man who had provided his ideal retreat to find out something about him. The inscription below the statue read: *To the undying memory of Augustus Rowley, visionary, philosopher and man of letters. Born* 1833: *died* 1873 *of languishment and a profound melancholy. He here awaits the vindication of time and circumstance, secure in the belief that he accurately interpreted the call of his Maker.*

Greville had been amused by the wordy epitaph, which he suspected had been written by Augustus Rowley himself. And, indeed, he had reason to be grateful to that obscure and pathetic dilettante, for the cottage on the island in a lake that was itself the creation of some previous Rowley had proved to be an ideal lair for a solitary transnormal in the transnormal world of the late twentieth century.

Indulging a whim, Greville had cut down the weeds that were scrambling vigorously round the grave of Augustus. Occasionally he would visit the churchyard and indulge in one-sided conversations with the extinct visionary, philosopher and man of letters. He took especial pleasure in trying to explain to the mute and invisible Augustus the present state of a world that, in the nineteenth century, must then have seemed to be the still point, the fixed centre of a turning universe. He had a happy feeling that if Augustus could really have appreciated the catastrophe that had overtaken his secure and well-ordered cosmos, it would have been quite enough to make that man of letters turn from the exquisite sculpture of his deathless sonnets to the quarry-like blastings of free verse.

Now, as Greville sat in the car with Liz and gazed at the battered lines of Waterloo Bridge, one span of which had been almost demolished by unknown causes and about which there lay a wreckage of small craft, and some quite sizeable pleasure boats, he was reminded of Augustus Rowley's certain conviction of immortality. *Sic transit gloria mundi* ... This is the way the world ends, not with a bang but a whimper.

"You are miles away," said Liz. "Where the hell are you?"

He looked at her with a start and realised that she had finished eating. She had also emptied her bottle of beer.

"Sorry," said Greville. He lifted his own bottle to his lips and drank from it gratefully. He suddenly felt very thirsty. "Would you like another bottle? There's a crate in the back of the car."

"No, thank you ... What were you thinking about? Were you wondering what to do with me?"

"No. That problem's settled, at least. I'm taking you back to Norfolk. If you make yourself agreeable, I might even eventually let you go chasing off after your sister Jane."

"And if I don't make myself agreeable?"

"Then I might toss you back to the dogs."

"Oh, well," said Liz equably and obscurely, "while there's a choice, life is not without interest ... Now, what were you thinking about? You had a sort of sad, faraway look in your eyes."

"Augustus Rowley," he said, "and mortality."

Then he told her about the cottage on the island and about Augustus Rowley's grave and the tiny ghost-like village of Ambergreave.

"It sounds all right," remarked Liz non-committally, when he had finished, "and Norfolk's on the way to Lancashire, so maybe I'm not doing too badly."

"You could have done considerably worse about an hour ago," Greville reminded her. "So don't take anything too much for granted."

"When are we going back?" she asked.

"Today. Now, in fact."

"I thought you were on the scrounge."

He pointed to the untidy heap of assorted goods in the back of the station wagon. "I did quite a bit of scrounging yesterday. I've got enough to be going on with."

"Oh." She seemed disappointed.

"What's the matter?"

"I wanted to see a bit of London. The last time I was here I was hardly more than a kid."

"There's nothing much to see," he said flatly. "Nothing but death and destruction, dogs, rats and a million broken windows."

"If we looked around a bit, you might find something you needed," said Liz hopefully.

Greville smiled. She was as eager and as pathetic as a child trying to talk an adult into giving it an outing.

"All right," he capitulated. "You can have a couple of hours. Then it's back to Norfolk. I can't risk any night driving."

"Greville, you're my kind of transie," she said gleefully. "And any time you feel like a good screw—" she pulled a face"—I mean, any time you wish to engage in carnal distraction, just make a noise."

He laughed. "Where do you want to go to first?"

"The Festival Hall. About ten centuries ago, I was taken to a concert there—a piano recital by a Hungarian called Georgie Sniffles, or something like that. He was marvellous. I always remembered it."

"Waterloo Bridge doesn't look too healthy," Greville pointed out.

"Aren't there any other bridges?"

He started the car, turned it round and went back to Westminster Bridge. Presently, after having made various detours round blocked streets, he pulled up outside the Festival Hall. Liz jumped out happily.

"Careful," he warned. "There may be a brigade of livestock lurking inside.

"Nonsense," said Liz. "There's nothing to eat here, except maybe a few hundredweight of sheet music."

Nevertheless, Greville loaded his shot-gun and then rummaged in the back of the station wagon until he found a single-barrel four-ten, which he gave to Liz with a handful of cartridges. He also gave her a battery powered torch.

"It's going to be dark inside," he said. "But don't use the torch more than you need. Dry cells that still work are hard to come by these days."

The Festival Hall seemed like a great derelict barn. Broken glass lay around in profusion. As they passed through the main doorway, they left the bright morning sunlight behind and entered a deep necropolitan gloom. The thin pencil beam of the torch probed a scene of desolation. Much of the wood panelling had been ripped away—presumably for fuel—and even the banisters of the main staircase had been hacked to pieces.

Liz, determined not to be oppressed by the destruction, began to hum tunelessly to herself. She led the way up the stairs, hesitating only momentarily when she had to step over a clean-picked skeleton still wearing the tattered remains of a printed dress like a grotesquely gay shroud.

"Rats," said Greville, as the torch beam hovered briefly over the sad heap of bones.

"Where?" whispered Liz apprehensively.

"I don't mean here and now. But *that's* the work of rats. Dogs would have crunched the bones. So would the kind of cats that have managed to survive . . . Let's get out. This place is too depressing."

"I want to see the hall," protested Liz. "I want to see where Georgie Sniffles had his grand piano, and I want to imagine all the people—the fat old ladies, the men in dinner jackets, the boys in brown corduroy, and all those girls in silk and taffeta rustling like a million grasshoppers."

"If you hear any rustling," retorted Greville, "shoot first and have visions afterwards. Rats don't make allowances for nostalgia."

Eventually they groped their way into the auditorium, a vault so black and so still that it seemed as if no sound at all—and certainly not music—could have disturbed its slumber for a thousand years. Strangely, there was not much damage. Here and there seats had been slashed, or clawed; and there was an overwhelming mustiness. But apart from cobwebs and mildew, the hall was structurally intact.

Liz shone the torch on the stage—and gave a small cry of wonder; for the last performance ever given in the Festival Hall had been The Nutcracker ballet. And the backcloth, frayed and tattered, was still miraculously hanging. Great faded Russian fir trees still loomed magically in the crystal forests dreamed of by Tchaikovsky. A few scatterings of paper snow—or rat leavings

—lay carelessly on the bare boards; and it seemed for a moment as if the lights might go up, the music begin, and the bright figure of the Snow Queen float gracefully from behind black velvet drapes.

"Oh! Isn't that absolutely wonderful!" breathed Liz. "You can almost feel it—after all these terrible years."

Suddenly, she dropped the torch and began to sob.

"Come on," said Greville in a voice that was purposefully harsh. "You've seen enough. We're getting out of here."

He picked up the torch and guided the still sobbing Liz away from the fir trees and the pathetic and enduring snow. As they went down the stairs he wondered if, before the rats came, the skeleton lying bleakly under its covering of printed cotton had also seen Tchaikovsky's fir trees and the paper snow of history. Perhaps the sad little skeleton had even danced upon that very stage. Perhaps it had once been a prima ballerina. Perhaps ... He cut off the thoughts before they could develop further.He did not want to know about the past any more. All he wanted—and all Liz wanted—was the blessed sunlight.

As they returned to it, the summer morning seemed incredibly sweet. They could not have been inside the Festival Hall more than about ten minutes. But to Greville it had seemed more like ten years. Slowly, Liz was recovering herself.

"Maybe it would be better if we cut out the sightseeing and headed for Norfolk," said Greville gently. "There's not very much left in London now—apart from ghosts and scavengers."

However, despite her recent tears, Liz was not to be deterred. "I may never come here again," she said. "I may get myself killed or swallowed up in the north ... London was such a lovely exciting city, wasn't it? I want to store up a few memories to tell all the grandchildren I'll most likely never have ... Besides, you promised. You promised me a couple of hours. You wouldn't go back on your promise, would you?"

Greville sighed. "I suppose you wouldn't be a transie if you didn't like banging your head on a wall. Where to next?"

"The centre of the universe," said Liz, suddenly gay.

"Piccadilly Circus. We'll sit in the Lyon's Corner House, and drink coffee and watch all the people going to work."

Greville drove the car back over Westminster Bridge, along the Embankment and up Northumberland Avenue. When they reached Trafalgar Square, it seemed momentarily like the day after a stupendous carnival or an orgy on the grand scale. There were two or three buses—one of them overturned—a cluster of taxis straddling the entry to the Strand, and an assortment of private cars large and small. Also there were people, lying about with careless abandon as if they were too drunk to move, as if they might have been celebrating some momentous occasion—such as the end of a war to end all wars.

The only trouble was, nothing moved. Nothing except the pigeons. For the pigeons were still there. With the conditioning of decades behind them, they would probably continue to haunt Trafalgar Square long after the last Londoner was dead.

Even as Liz and Greville glanced at the scene, the aftermath of the carnival resolved itself into a sunlit nightmare. The buses were rusty hulks, the taxis had been cannibalised for spare parts—even wheels and radiators—and some of the cars had been riddled with small-arms fire. The drunks—men, women and a few children—were no more than tattered rag-doll skeletons, lying where they had fallen, some of them with rusty guns cradled like strange talismans in arms that were only whitened bones.

And only the pigeons moved. They had been feeding (even pigeons had adapted to the new order—and a new diet) or basking or squabbling or merely strutting importantly among the buses. But the sound of the car had disturbed them; and they rose angrily and noisily up into the morning sunlight, whirling past the high effigy of Nelson, who still stood on his column and stared serenely ahead with his wide blind eyes.

A shot rang out. A chip of roadway sprang up in front of the station wagon.

"I thought there might be one or two about!" snapped Greville obscurely. He slammed the car into first gear and accelerated. Another bullet ricocheted plaintively where a moment ago the station wagon had been standing.

Greville drove skilfully round the overturned bus, zigzagged among the wrecked small cars and then found a clear run through Cockspur Street and the Haymarket.

Piccadilly Circus presented much the same kind of petrified desolation as Trafalgar Square, except that two massive army tanks blocked the entry to Regent Street, and Eros—the frail statue which had once seemed like an irresistible magnet for hundreds of thousands of Londoners—had been blown to glory.

Piccadilly Circus had obviously been the scene of a pitched battle. The carnage was heavier than in Trafalgar Square, and tattered remnants of uniforms still hung over the disorderly heaps of bones. The front of the London Pavilion had been shot to pieces and so had Swan and Edgars. The main entrance to the Piccadilly Tube Station was merely a pile of rubble; and large pieces of masonry lay scattered among the bones and wrecked cars that blocked the entrances to Piccadilly and Shaftesbury Avenue.

"Satisfied?" demanded Greville harshly.

Liz nodded, her face white.

"Right. Now we can get the hell out of here and go to a place where it's still relatively pleasant to live."

"Please," she said. "There's just one thing more I'd like to see ... It—it means quite a lot. I want to go to the British Museum. It's all tied up with being a little girl and feeling safe and secure in a fairly normal world ... My father used to go there a lot. He took me once or twice when I was about nine ... Do you think we could take a quick look?"

"If we don't get ambushed on the way," retorted Greville grimly. "But that's the last stop. After that, we're off to Norfolk."

"Yes," sighed Liz. "That's the last stop."

Greville took the car along Coventry Street. He drove slowly. There were what looked like several miniature shell-holes in the scarred roadway, and the passing of the station wagon raised clouds of fine dust from the rubble.

# SIX

So far, they had not encountered any human being—unless one could include the brief sniping in Trafalgar Square—but it was still quite early in the morning; and the "normal" transnormal would give the rats and cats and other nocturnal scroungers plenty of time to disperse before he ventured forth. However, as the car turned up Charing Cross Road, Liz and Greville saw their first transie of the day—an old man almost bent double under the weight of an obviously heavy sack over his shoulder.

He took one glance at the car, dropped the sack and scuttled like a frightened rabbit. Out of curiosity, Greville pulled up by the sack and inspected its contents.

"What is it?" asked Liz.

"Tinned goods." Greville looked along the road, but the old man was nowhere to be seen. He might still be lurking in a doorway or he might have decided to abandon his spoils rather than risk being shot. There was no way of knowing.

Greville opened the rear door of the station wagon and lifted the sack. "It would be a pity to leave this lot, wouldn't it?"

"What if he comes back?" asked Liz.

"What if he doesn't?"

Finally they compromised by taking half the tins—mostly fruit juices, but there was also a tin of sausages and beans—and leaving the rest in the sack on the roadway.

"I'm surprised the rats haven't chewed the labels off," said Greville. "The old boy must have found them in a rat-proof cellar, somewhere."

"Or maybe," said Liz, "they were just tucked away in an old fridge."

Having stowed away the dozen or so tins they had acquired, they set off once more towards the British Museum. Unlike Piccadilly Circus and Trafalgar Square,

St. Giles's Circus was hardly damaged, and they crossed Oxford Street without any difficulty. Even in Great Russell Street, there was nothing to impede their progress but a very few old skeletons without even a rag of clothing in the vicinity. In life, thought Greville as he drove past the pathetic remains, they might well have been a bunch of crackpot nudists. Anything was possible in a transnormal world. But what was more probable was that the corpses had been stripped to provide clothing for the living.

Outside, the British Museum seemed completely unchanged—as if it still proposed to endure for ever. But inside, the massive building was a ruin.

In the library, the works of Shakespeare, Dostoevsky, Jung and Einstein—along with obscure medieval chronicles, twentieth-century text-books of nuclear physics, histories of witchcraft and political philosophies—all had been converted into a vast cosmopolis of nests for vermin. Fortunately, the nests were old, the vermin had departed to make new conquests. But their half-digested droppings of Dante and Ouida, Homer and Silas K. Hocking remained.

The British Museum stank. And the stench was of decay and death, and blind and bloody futility. But, also, there were piles of charred books and smoke blackened ceilings. Testimony, perhaps to the empty revenge of a few transnormals on the culture that had formerly rejected them. Or perhaps merely the work of homeless and starving children who had made fires to ward off evil spirits, emboldened animals and the bitter cold of darkness—until the rats took over.

But the devastation was not confined to the library. In the Egyptian Room the massive stone statue of Rameses still stood, defying rats, beetles, transnormals and time itself. But elsewhere the destructibles had been destroyed, the combustibles had been burnt, the eatables had been eaten.

As Greville surveyed the gloomy immensity of halls and galleries, he was surprised at how much of history could be eaten—and probably not only by insects and animals. But then, he reflected grimly, life was essentially cannibalistic. Cultures and societies consumed each other, as well as animals and men . . .

Liz had been silent. Unnaturally silent. She merely held his hand tightly like a small child. A frightened child. No father now to reassure her, no discreet whispers of ordinary people patronising the relics of the centuries with tepid and sophisticated curiosity. Only gothic halls of desolation and the almost tangible silence of the dead that have been made to die yet again.

In the dull light, Greville suddenly noticed that Liz seemed very pale and withdrawn. For a while he had been so absorbed in the mute tragedy around him, that he had barely given her a thought. But now he suddenly realised that it would be a good thing to get her outside as quickly as possible—out into the morning sunlight.

"Come on," he said. "You've already seen too much."

She seemed only to be able to stop herself from running with a tremendous effort. Out in the blessed sunlight once more, she heaved a great sigh of relief. And fainted on the steps.

Greville caught her. After a minute or two her colour came back, and he gave her a bottle of beer.

"Well, you got what you wanted. You've seen the sights," he said drily. "Shall we put a few miles behind us?"

She nodded. "I'm sorry. I thought—I thought . . ."

"You thought it was all going to be sad and terribly romantic," he interrupted roughly. "Well, it isn't. It's mean and it's dirty and it's downright ugly . . . Now, if you aren't going to be sick or anything like that, let's get in the car and start moving."

After half an hour's driving, involving several small detours, Greville took the station wagon cautiously along Old Street and into Shoreditch, where he hit the A10. Then he picked up speed. Driving along the trunk road was easier but more dangerous, for trunk-road districts were the main hunting grounds of most "foreign" scroungers.

Liz still remained withdrawn. She slumped in the passenger seat and stared listlessly at the road ahead. Greville had been a little surprised by her reactions both at the Festival Hall and at the British Museum. From what he knew of her recent existence, he would have thought that she would be able to take the disintegration of London landmarks in her stride. But then, he reflected, the city she remembered would have been a bright, imaginary city of childhood. Despite her "cloistered" life in Richmond—perhaps even because of it—she had probably cherished the happy illusion that things could not be quite so bad in what was once one of the great cities of the world.

Apart from the old man who had dropped his sack and fled, they did not encounter any other transnormals in the journey across London. Greville was agreeably surprised. He did not harbour many illusions about his fellow transnormals, and knew that a well-laden car complete with provisions, guns and ammunition would be regarded by a lot of people as a prize worth taking risks for. He drove with a pistol handy and a loaded shot-gun across his knees. If he could help it, he was not going to be taken by surprise.

But it was still quite early in the day and, apart from thoughts of plunder, there was no reason why any transnormals should bestir themselves. Later, no doubt, probably towards noon, London's dwindling inhabitants would waken up and venture abroad. But by that time he would be clear of the city and on the relatively easy road to Cambridge.

As the car passed without much difficulty through Hackney, Stoke Newington and Tottenham, Greville's spirits rose. It was a fine summer morning and, despite his alcoholic rendezvous on Chelsea Bridge the night before, he was feeling good. Soon he would be back in Ambergreave; and with Liz—well, at least he would have someone to talk to. And, if required—to use her own description—someone to screw. However, sex was a problem that had not really bothered him for some time. In a detached sort of way, he wondered if it still mattered.

"How old are you?" asked Liz suddenly. Her colour was coming back, and she looked as if she was beginning to revive.

Greville had to think for a moment. "Thirty-seven," he said at last. "Why?"

Liz smiled. "I wondered about the white hair."

"It turned overnight," said Greville solemnly, "with the shock of discovering that I had reached puberty."

They both laughed, and the laughter seemed to disperse much of the tension that had been building up.

The ambush did not come until they had almost reached the small town of Ware, thirty miles north of London.

It came on a dull, dead suburban road where most of the gardens and privet hedges of semi-detached houses were so overgrown that the houses themselves were nearly lost to view.

It came in the shape of an old truck that suddenly hurtled out of a side-road and blocked Greville's path. He braked, swerved and tried to drive round it. But the ambushers had chosen their spot well. The road was too narrow.

To avoid a collision, Greville stamped on the brake pedal and brought his station wagon to a halt with the front wings just touching the rear of the truck. Before he could reach for his gun, the privet hedges on either side of the road parted, displaying at least four rifles or shot-guns already covering him.

A figure stepped out of the hedge on the near side. It was brandishing an old army-type revolver.

"Don't do anything neurotic," piped a thin voice, "unless you feel like having your face spread all over the windscreen."

Greville kept his hands on the wheel and let out an audible sigh. Then he gazed through the open side window at the cheerfully lethal expression on the face of a boy of perhaps sixteen.

## SEVEN

THE ambushers came out from behind the hedges that had concealed them and stood warily round the car. The driver of the truck jumped down and joined them. Somebody lit a cigarette, somebody laughed. They seemed extraordinarily pleased with themselves. Altogether there were half a dozen of them; and none of them looked to be more than about eighteen.

The boy with the revolver was not laughing. There

were tiny beads of sweat on his face, and he seemed to have trouble containing a tremendous and subtle excitement. Greville looked at his eyes—blue, piercing and at the same time oddly remote—and knew that they were the eyes of a killer.

The revolver waved negligently. "All right, Uncle," said the thin, high-pitched voice, "get out of the car very slowly because we're all terribly nervous, and our fingers have a habit of twitching when we get the least bit upset."

This injunction was met with a guffaw by one of the other boys. "Good old Nibs! He's a real way-out Charlie!"

Nibs glanced at the speaker. "Shove it, Smiler. My sense of humour has a low sugar content."

The words were spoken very quietly, but as he got out of the car Greville noticed that Smiler seemed to shrink visibly.

"And now let us observe your esteemed lady companion in all her glory," said Nibs. He waved the revolver towards Liz. "Come on, now, move your hot little bottom."

Liz and Greville exchanged glances. Neither of them could read anything at all in the other's eyes. Liz seemed unnaturally calm. Thank God for that, thought Greville. One little wrong thing and these kids would start shooting just for the hell of it.

Liz got out of the car very slowly.

Greville turned to Nibs. "What do you want?" he said evenly.

Nibs lifted the revolver fractionally until it was pointing at Greville's stomach. "Say sir."

"Sir."

Suddenly Nibs leaned forward, put out his free hand and slapped Greville's face hard. "Say thank you."

Greville immediately suppressed the impulse that rose in him. He knew that Nibs wanted to kill him. He thought he could get the gun, and he thought it would take all of ten seconds to break the boy in two. But there were other guns. And there was Liz.

"Thank you—sir."

"That's better, Uncle. Now go down on your knees and beg my forgiveness for asking tiresome questions."

Greville got down on his knees, not daring to look at Liz. One of the boys sniggered. "That Nibs. He has style, man. Real style."

"I beg your forgiveness, sir," said Greville quietly. He was thinking: so long as this kid can show them how big he is by using me as a door-mat, he'll let me stay alive.

"That's better, Uncle. We begin to understand each other. You may kiss my shoes."

Greville kissed his shoes. Nibs lightly kicked his face for the privilege. The rest of the gang found this excruciatingly funny.

"Stand up, Uncle. You're overdoing it."

Greville stood up. Nibs spat in his face.

"Thank you, sir."

"Uncle," said Nibs, "you're bright. But don't let it go to your head."

"No, sir."

"Now what kind of treasures have you got in your nice little motor-car?"

"Guns, ammunition, some shirts, woodworking tools, a crate of beer and a few books."

Nibs slapped him again. "You forgot to say sir."

"Sorry, sir."

"It looks to me, Uncle," said Nibs pleasantly, "as if you might have come by your little haul somewhat dishonestly. That is not nice, is it?"

"No, sir."

Nibs glanced at his companions and sighed. "My dears! What is the older generation coming to?" There was a gust of laughter. Nibs turned to Greville once more.

"I hope you are bitterly sorry for your sins."

"Yes, sir."

"Repeat after me: I am filled with remorse and penitence."

"I am filled with remorse and penitence, sir."

"I am very distressed by your recent lack of honesty, Uncle," said Nibs solemnly. "I know the temptations are great in this wicked world, but you should try to be strong. You didn't try hard enough, did you?"

"No, sir."

"Then you must try much harder in future—if you

have a future. Meanwhile purely in the interests of justice, we shall have to confiscate this little lot. Firearms are particularly dangerous in the hands of inexperienced persons."

Greville was beginning to understand how Nibs had become the leader of a gang of boys most of whom were older and stronger than he was. The boy, despite his weak face and effeminate voice, had brains and a literally striking personality. He also had a sure feeling for his audience. At the moment, the other boys were hanging on his every word and enjoying themselves hugely. Through Nibs, no doubt, and on the person of Greville they were wreaking vengeance for the lost security of a world that had simply gone from bad to worse throughout the major part of their young lives.

Most of them had probably been orphaned years ago, and they could only have survived by good luck and sheer singlemindedness. Greville could imagine the kind of terrifying problems with which they would have had to cope. Objectively, he could be sorry for them all. Subjectively, he felt like killing them—particularly Nibs—with his bare hands.

So far, Liz had done nothing except watch Greville make his bid for survival by passively accepting whatever form of abasement the boys cared to thrust on him. In the bright sunshine she thought his face looked tired and old. A good deal older than thirty-seven. She felt sorry for him. She felt sorry for herself too. She thought he was underestimating Nibs and his confederates. She thought they were both going to be killed anyway. She thought it would be a good idea to try to take one or two of these nasty little transies with them. All she needed from Greville was a sign. But there was no sign. Nothing at all.

Then Nibs was talking again. "Now, Uncle, having satisfactorily disposed of the burden of your worldly possessions, let us consider your only remaining problem. What about hot bottom, here?" He gave Liz a look of moist malevolence.

"She's my woman—sir."

"Your wife?"

Greville thought quickly about that one. "No." He collected another slap. "No, sir."

Nibs was really enjoying himself. "Uncle, you distress me. Not content with stealing, you also have an unwholesome taste for fornication . . . That is very naughty. Repeat after me: I am a dirty old man."

"I am a dirty old man, sir."

"Do you repent of this sordid fornication?"

Greville hesitated, and the gun barrel rose again. "Yes, sir."

"I'm pleased to hear it. We shall remove the temptation." He turned to Liz. "Take off your clothes, dearest. We wish to inspect the charms that have turned poor Uncle here into a sinful old gentleman."

Liz did not move. She looked past him, trying not to think.

"Big Ears," said Nibs, addressing a dullish youth who was at least as tall as Greville and probably about twenty pounds heavier, "help the lady to disrobe."

Big Ears grinned, laid down his shot-gun and took hold of Liz. She kicked him. Big Ears laughed and hit her in the stomach. Liz groaned and doubled up. Big ears pushed her to the ground and rolled her on her back. Then he tore her blue shirt open from neck to waist.

Liz kicked him again, and again he hit her in the stomach. Then he ripped the shirt off over her head, leaving her panting and groaning.

"All right?" said Big Ears, looking at Nibs.

"For the moment." Nibs was watching Greville and relishing the situation.

"She's a proper little playmate," said Big Ears. He scooped Liz up almost fondly and set her on her feet. "There's still quite a bit of mileage left in her, I shouldn't wonder."

"Yes," said Nibs, still looking at Greville. "I imagine Uncle, here, hasn't ever tried her in top gear."

"She looks a pretty fair shag," said one of the other youths. "How about it, Nibs?"

"Let's have a go," added Big Ears almost pleadingly. "There's nothing else to do before we send 'em."

Nibs smiled. "Boys, whatever are you thinking of? Here am I trying to re-educate Uncle. Do you want to set him a bad example?"

There was a burst of laughter. Nibs turned to Greville

with a sigh, and shrugged. "Boys will be boys, Uncle . . . I do hope you will forgive their gay high spirits."

Greville said nothing. Nibs hit him and he still said nothing. He knew he wasn't going to be killed now until they had finished raping Liz. That gave him a little more time. What use it would be, he did not know. Probably they were both going to be killed anyway. He wondered cynically whether Liz would really prefer to die before or after. But he didn't look at her. He hadn't the courage.

"Uncle is sulking," said Nibs. "Let's see what we can do to cheer him up . . . Smiler, you and Big Ears and Mumbles can play with darlingest on the lawn for a few minutes—and don't make it longer than five each because Jim-Jim and Lookers won't be very happy if there isn't much left . . . Jim-Jim, move the truck in case we have visitors. Lookers, you can help me entertain Uncle until Smiler and Co. have got rid of their problems."

Liz began to fight, but she could do nothing at all against Smiler, Big Ears and Mumbles. They lifted her bodily and took her behind one of the overgrown privet hedges where nothing more exciting than a weekly mowing and a spring planting had happened for nearly half a century. They dumped Liz in the now long grass. Mumbles held her arms, Smiler pulled her trousers down and Big Ears prepared himself to take the first ride.

Liz suddenly stopped struggling. What the hell was the use? But she didn't close her eyes. As Big Ears lay on top of her, forcing her legs apart and rhythmically exciting himself by noting her pain reaction as he pinched and pulled the nipple of her left breast, she tried to will her body not to respond, tried to pretend the pain belonged to someone else. He bit her lip, forcing her mouth open against his. But still she did not close her eyes. She gazed into his, clouded and vacant with lust, hating him, willing him to die. He didn't. He just worked stolidly and mindlessly towards a crude mechanical climax.

Meanwhile, Jim-Jim got back into the truck and backed it into the side road, while Lookers sat on the edge of the pavement and cradled his two-two rifle with the barrel pointing generally in Greville's direction. And Greville did nothing.

Now that his active force had been temporarily reduced, Nibs handled his revolver carefully. He stood two paces back from Greville. He was taking no chances.

Nibs listened eagerly to the subdued noises behind the hedge. Occasionally, there was a grunt. Occasionally, Liz could not avoid letting out a low animal moan. Nibs smiled. The beads of sweat became larger on his downy upper lip. He was getting more sensual pleasure out of the situation than if he had been on top of Liz himself.

Much more, thought Greville. For besides being a killer Nibs was a sadist. God alone knew what had happened to him to turn him into what he was. It must have been something pretty ghastly. Or a whole lot of things that were pretty ghastly ... He tried not to think about Liz ... He tried only to think of a way of getting a gun before he himself was shot.

Still keeping his revolver trained on Greville, Nibs took a quick look over the hedge. "Big Ears has finished," he said conversationally. "Your dear lady looks as if she's enjoying it, Uncle. You must have been starving her. Never mind, she ought to have a pretty full belly by the time old Mumbles has finished with her. Mumbles doesn't say much, but he's got talent."

Jim-Jim, gun in hand, had returned from parking the truck."I can hear something," he said.

Nibs laughed. "It's only hot bottom having fun. Smiler's on the job."

"No. I mean a car engine. Listen."

They listened.

"It's a car all right," said Lookers, rising briefly into eloquence. "Shall we let it through, Nibs? We got a nice enough haul for one day."

But Nibs was drunk with power. "Not on your nelly." He peered over the hedge. "Let Smiler finish his ride by himself. She isn't going to stand up and cheer. The rest of us are going into routine. There's another one, coming." He turned back to Greville. "Come across the road, Uncle, and lie down—unless you want to have it now."

Greville walked obediently across the road and lay

down in a gateway, while Nibs stood behind him. Jim-Jim had disappeared and was already gunning the truck's engine. As far as a casual observer was concerned, the road was deserted—except for a station wagon apparently parked at a crazy angle to the kerb.

Greville permitted himself to hope a little. Not too much, but a little. If only the car that was coming contained two or three well-armed men!

For about a hundred yards the road was straight. Then there was a slight bend. Nibs had chosen his spot carefully. It was not the kind of road where you would expect trouble. It was suburban, dead, uninteresting.

Suddenly the oncoming car appeared round the bend. It was an ancient Land Rover with tarpaulin covers over the back. Nibs raised an arm. Someone on the other side of the road repeated the signal. Jim-Jim brought the truck roaring out of the side road. There was a screeching of brakes as the Land Rover pulled up.

It's now or never, thought Greville. But Nibs had anticipated him. Even as he leaped to his feet the revolver came crashing on to the back of his head. He blacked out and went down again. By the time he returned to consciousness, the driver of the Land Rover was already out of his car and being interrogated by Nibs and Big Ears. Mumbles was standing beside Greville, his rifle ready and a benign expression on his face.

Greville's hopes faded rapidly. The driver of the Land Rover wore the long black habit of a priest.

## EIGHT

In almost any other situation the priest would have been a comic figure. As it was, he seemed pathetic and grotesque. He was a plump, bald man of about fifty. He faced the four homicidal youths who barred his path with an odd mixture of bewilderment and self-confidence.

However, his reactions must be reasonably fast, thought Greville, for he had managed to stop his car much quicker than Greville had done. The Land Rover now lay about ten yards behind Greville's station wagon; and the fat priest had come ambling towards the boys almost eagerly, as if he simply could not see the guns that were pointed at him. So eager did he seem to be that he literally fell over himself and appeared to twist an ankle—to the intense amusement of Nibs, Big Ears, Jim-Jim and Lookers.

Smiler was still behind the hedge with Liz, working steadily to his appointed end and at the same time trying to make up his mind whether she had really fainted or was just shamming. Mumbles, despite the diversion in the roadway, kept his eyes on Greville. He wasn't taking any chances at all.

The priest got to his feet, winced with pain, limped a couple of steps and then sat down again. He looked up at Nibs, squinting against the sunlight.

"Good morning, father," said Nibs. "God be with you."

"My son, what on earth are you playing silly tricks for? If I hadn't managed to brake quickly I might have suffered a very serious injury. I might even have been killed ... As it is, I doubt very much whether I shall be able to do any more driving today. My leg hurts abominably, and my nerves are quite shaken."

This little speech was greeted by a gale of laughter.

"Be consoled, father," said Nibs. "I shouldn't be at all surprised if you haven't just been granted a Sign. God moves mysteriously, I believe. He may even have decided to terminate your driving career altogether."

Nibs was clearly at the top of his form. His remarks provoked more laughter, and Big Ears seemed to be on the point of having a convulsion.

"My son," said the priest indignantly, "it does not do to mock the cloth."

"I stand reproved," said Nibs. "Now, fat arse, what have you got in the back of your agony wagon?"

The priest blinked. "Nothing, I'm afraid, but two poor children ... Please don't frighten them. They're rather sensitive."

Nibs turned to Lookers. "Go and get an eyeful. Fat arse may be playing games."

"Please!" said the priest. He seemed to be trying to

stand up again. But Lookers had almost reached the Land Rover.

Then miracles began to happen thick and fast.

In a loud voice, the priest shouted, "Now!" At the same time, he simultaneously launched himself at Nibs, grabbing him round the knees and bringing him down, revolver and all.

While that was happening, Mumbles momentarily took his eyes away from Greville. It wasn't much of a chance, thought Greville, but it was the best he was likely to get. He rolled over, grabbed the nearest foot and threw Mumbles off balance. The boy tried to bring his rifle round, but Greville held the barrel; and a bullet ricocheted peevishly along the road. Then Mumbles was down. All Greville's pent up fury broke loose. With one hand, he grabbed the boy's throat, lifted him bodily and brought his head crashing back against the hard pavement. Mumbles sighed and lay still.

Meanwhile, from somewhere in the back of the Land Rover, a sub-machine gun chattered loudly and briefly. Lookers clutched his stomach, spun like a top and fell. The same burst swept by to include Jim-Jim and Big Ears. Jim-Jim ran three paces then doubled up and lay twitching and screaming. Big Ears just stared—a look of utter disbelief on his face—as blood spurted from his neck and chest. Then he slumped soundlessly forward.

"Enough!" shouted the priest. He was lying on top of Nibs, whose arm was twisted behind his back and whose face was pressed into the roadway. The priest had his revolver. He was pointing it at Smiler's white startled face which had just appeared over the top of the hedge.

Greville raised his own arms quickly. He didn't want to get shot by mistake. "That's all of them," he called. "You've got the lot."

The priest's eyes—no longer weak or comic—flickered briefly towards him. "Keep your hands up," he said. "We don't want any silly mistakes, do we?" He turned to Smiler once more. "Now, smart boy, come through that hedge very slowly—if you want to live a little longer."

Smiler forced his way through the hedge. His trousers were hanging round his ankles. He made a move to pull them up, but the priest said: "Dress will be informal. Stay still!"

Smiler stayed still.

"Look," said Greville, "they've been raping my girl. She's behind the hedge. Can I go to her?"

"Charming," said the priest. "Stay still. What about the one you got?"

"I belted his head," said Greville. "He's still breathing."

The priest called towards the Land Rover: "All right, children, come out."

The tail gate was lowered and two girls—neither of whom could have been more than twenty—got out. One carried a shot-gun, and the other an automatic rifle.

"Are you all right, Father Jack?" asked the girl with the shot-gun.

"Quite all right, my dear," said Father Jack, standing up. He turned to Greville once more. "Collect all the hardware," he indicated the weapons lying by Smiler, Jim-Jim, Big Ears and Lookers, "and don't be clever. Put them in the middle of the road. Then you can see whether your girl is still with us."

Greville did as he was told. Then he went into the tiny little garden where Liz had been taken.

She lay as Smiler had left her, in the long grass. She was completely naked and looked as if she had taken a hell of a beating; but she was still conscious. One of her eyes was badly bruised and almost closed up. There was blood running from a swollen lip and teeth marks all over her shoulders and breasts. There were two wide yellowish-blue patches on her belly.

She recognised Greville, tried to smile and couldn't. "I told you I wasn't much good for anything but screwing," she whispered hoarsely, so low that he could hardly hear. Then suddenly, she rolled over and was violently sick.

Greville knelt and supported her shivering retching body. "Oh, Liz! I brought you into a real dose of trouble, didn't I?" He wanted to comfort her and murmur stupid tender things, but all the words were frozen inside him.

Presently, she stopped vomiting. He gathered her

torn shirt and trousers and helped her to put them on. Then he hunted for her shoes and found that they had been thrown under the hedge.

She tried to stand up. She could get to her feet, but she couldn't stand upright. Nor could she move. Greville picked her up gently and carried her out of the garden. He took her to the station wagon and laid her on the passenger seat. Tears were trickling down her face, but the crying was soundless and without any movement. He found some brandy and offered it to her, but she just turned her head away.

Greville closed the car door and went towards Father Jack. Despite the cassock, Father Jack did not look at all like a priest now. He seemed to have grown visibly thinner and taller. No longer a comic figure, he looked tough and purposeful.

Mumbles had returned to consciousness, and Father Jack had lined him up with Nibs and Smiler, whose trousers were still round his ankles. The three youths had their hands on top of their heads.

As Greville left Liz one of Father Jack's "children" went to her. The other kept her automatic rifle pointing at the three boys. With the revolver that he had acquired from Nibs, Father Jack administered the *coup de grace* to Jim-Jim, who had not stopped screaming from the moment he was hit. The shot rang out and Jim-Jim's screams ended abruptly.

The silence that followed seemed extraordinary—something far more subtle than a mere absence of sound.

"Well, now," said Father Jack, "we live in exciting times, don't we? How did you come to get mixed up with these bad lads?"

"The same way as you," said Greville and told him what had happened.

When he had finished, Father Jack looked at Nibs thoughtfully. "I'm beginning to think that you are a shade anti-social, my son."

"Shove the crap," said Nibs. "You were lucky, but that's the way it goes. Today, you, tomorrow somebody else. Nobody gives a damn about anything. Why should they? We're all bleeding nuts." Nibs was pale but his voice was steady.

Suddenly, Greville felt bitterly sorry for him. Suddenly, Nibs was not just a boy psychopath: he was all of mankind. He was the human tragedy writ small . . . He was also a homicidal sadist . . .

At that moment, Mumbles rose to a brief eloquence. He had been standing there with a dazed expression on his face and blood trickling steadily down his neck from the head wound he had gained when Greville slammed him against the stone pavement.

"I want to say something," said Mumbles. "You're going to kill us, I know that. But I want to say something. I want to say I'm sorry. Not just for this. Not for trying to get you, or screwing the girl or anything like that . . . I don't know what I want to say really . . . I just want to say I'm sorry . . . Maybe I'm sorry because it's such a bloody rotten world . . . Maybe I'm sorry because this is the one we lost." His voice broke. "I don't know. I'm just sorry, that's all. There's nothing else to it."

Father Jack gazed at him intently. 'That's a very interesting speech, my son. Kindly turn round. Your face saddens me a little."

Mumbles turned round obediently, presenting the back of his head to Father Jack. With a rapid movement, the priest lifted his revolver and hit Mumbles with it just below the base of the skull. Mumbles fell without uttering a sound.

"Now," said Father Jack, turning to Smiler and studying his partial nudity, "you appear to have been surprised *in flagrante delicto*. Have you any observations to make?"

"Go stuff yourself," retorted Smiler bravely.

Father Jack sighed. "*Ego te absolvo*, my son." He shot Smiler neatly through the forehead.

Nibs looked at the body, then he looked at Greville and finally at Father Jack. He licked his lips. "Father, can I confess before . . ." He looked at the gun and left the sentence unfinished.

"Confess away, my son."

"It's not that I believe any of the crap your lot hands out, you understand," went on Nibs calmly. "But my family was Catholic, see? It—it sort of brings us together a bit." He glanced once more at Greville. "If it's not too much trouble, I'd like it a bit private."

"Go down on your knees," said Father Jack. He turned to Greville. "Perhaps you will excuse us?"

Greville said nothing. He went back to the car and spoke to Liz. She even managed to smile at him. Then she closed her eyes and leaned back as if she wanted to do nothing at all but sleep.

Greville watched Father Jack and Nibs. The boy was on his knees in the roadway. He was talking quickly and quietly. Evidently, thought Greville, he had quite a lot to confess.

It lasted about five minutes. Then Father Jack laid his hand on the boy's forehead, and Nibs made the sign of the cross.

And almost immediately, he lunged at Father Jack's legs. The priest went down heavily, with Nibs scrabbling for the gun. He didn't get it.

"*Ego te absolvo,* my son," said Father Jack in a loud voice. The gun could not be seen. The sound of the shot was flat and muffled.

But Nibs was suddenly transformed from a killer making his last attempt at killing into a small and oddly pathetic heap. He rolled convulsively on to his back and lay still in the roadway. Just another dead boy. A late and indirect casualty of ten years of Omega radiation.

Father Jack picked himself up and shook the dust off. His limp had completely disappeared. "Well, now," he said, "perhaps we ought to look to the lady."

## NINE

FATHER JACK was not a Catholic priest—in fact, he had not been ordained as any kind of priest. For nearly twenty years he had been head gardener at the Convent of the Sacred Heart, near Newmarket. Before that he had been a convict, and before that he had been an unambitious and reasonably successful burglar. Before he became a burglar, he had served for five years as a paratrooper.

But now, as an almost natural result of all the years

of Omega radiation and the Radiant Suicide, he had become simply Father Jack. "Father" in the literal sense of the word, for he had polygamously married four of the oldest surviving girls at the convent and had already begotten half a dozen children.

At the beginning of the Radiant Suicide, the Convent of the Sacred Heart had a complement of one mother superior, eight teaching and working nuns, fifty girls, a head gardener, an assistant gardener and a general handyman. In the first two years, the assistant gardener, the handyman and two of the nuns committed suicide. Everyone else was enjoined to carry on as if nothing abnormal was happening; for there was still God's work to be done. A few of the girls were taken away by their parents, but most remained and were rapidly orphaned.

For many years the convent had been growing most of its own food; and so its occupants were able to keep going in a reasonably normal fashion until early in 1977. The trouble came one day when Father Jack—who was then still plain Jack Rowbottom—was out hunting for meat. It came, as trouble usually came, in the shape of a truckload of men out on the scrounge.

Jack Rowbottom had already taken the precaution of acquiring firearms and instructing the nuns in their use; so that, despite the fact that they were outnumbered by an enemy with superior firepower, the nuns gave a fairly good account of themselves. Meanwhile most of the girls took advantage of the escape route that had been thoughtfully provided for such an occasion at the cost of much sustained labour by the head gardener. It was an incredibly small tunnel which he had dug from the cellars of the convent to the outer wall of the kitchen garden. Immediately outside the wall there was a few acres of shrubs and woodland. The girls were supposed to scatter and hide among the trees until any trouble that arose had either passed by or been dealt with effectively.

Jack Rowbottom did not get back from his hunting expedition until the attack on the convent had ended and the attackers had gone away laden with spoils. The nuns were all dead of either bullet wounds or knife-wounds gained in the hand-to-hand fighting. The mother superior had been hanged from a banister, although judging from what had already happened to her the hanging could have no more than a symbolic value. A few of the girls were unlucky enough to go back to the convent too soon. A few more had been caught. They were raped and/or abducted or killed.

So Jack Rowbottom, left by himself with more than thirty adolescent girls and an odd sense of responsibility, inescapably became Father Jack—father extraordinary of the Convent of the Sacred Heart.

Provided they were left in peace, he thought he could train the girls to be reasonably self-sufficient. For most of them had already learned to help in the kitchen gardens and they could look after pigs and poultry. Some could weave, some were passing fair at carpentry and some could even cure bacon.

But obviously they were not going to be left alone. So Father Jack set about training them for survival. First he selected the six strongest and least nervous of the girls and formed them into a commando. Then he took them out raiding for weapons. The girls, though young, made rather good fighters since they had been accustomed to a rigorous discipline. Father Jack underlined the lesson of discipline and added to it the training in surprise attack and hand-to-hand combat that he himself had acquired as a paratrooper. Before he had finished, the girls could shoot, bayonet, throw knives, garotte, kick and gouge as good as most young soldiers and better than many.

They got their weapons. Then they set about converting the Convent of the Sacred Heart into a citadel. Then the commando was split up to train other commandos. And eventually Father Jack had nearly thirty girls, deceptively young, deceptively helpless, who were all trained fighters.

Occasionally he left the convent to go on scrounging expeditions, taking two or three of the girls with him. He was returning from one of these expeditions when Jim-Jim had blocked the road with his truck and had thus precipitated the fracas that had certainly saved Greville and Liz from being ultimately killed.

Greville learned all this about an hour after Nibs had been despatched and while they were taking a late lunch outside a solitary and deserted pub about half-way between Ware and Royston. In return, he gave Father Jack a succinct account of his own activities during the last ten years. But for some reason he could not understand, he translated Pauline's death into the death of a stranger. She became simply the driver of another fictitious car into which he had crashed while he was drunk. Father Jack accepted this version easily enough. There was no reason why he shouldn't.

There was nothing on either side of the pub at which they had stopped except a long rolling ribbon of road, carpeted here and there with patches of dandelion, nettles and convolvulus. There was nothing behind the pub except a wide vacancy of overgrown fields and sprawling hedges. That was why they had chosen it—because it was free from the possibility of surprise attack.

After Greville had collected up all the spare guns, and had then made Liz as comfortable as he could, they had driven away from the scene of the ambush slowly and in convoy, with Father Jack's battered Land Rover leading the way. Surprisingly, Liz did not appear to have suffered any lasting physical injury; but she was sore, pitifully sore and especially between her legs. Marilyn, the elder of Father Jack's "children", had examined Liz to the best of her limited ability. She arrived at the sensible conclusion that what Liz needed more than anything was a good hot bath and a long, lazy soak.

So here they were at the pub, whose cracked but still hanging signboard proclaimed it to be *The Angler's Rest*. Somewhere in its interior, the girls had found an old zinc bath full of the dusty and accumulated household debris of years. They had cleaned it up while Greville used a spanner to make one of the taps in the kitchen work. Eventually he managed to turn it, and out came a trickle of red, muddy water that presently grew into quite a fast flow and became relatively clear.

Meanwhile, Father Jack had taken a couple of portable paraffin stoves from his Land Rover and began to heat the water in a large jamming pan and an old five-gallon oil drum that had been discovered in the pub.

While all these preparations were going on Liz lay slumped in her seat in the station wagon. She looked even worse than she had done when Greville took her out of the garden after she had endured the attentions of Big Ears and Smiler; but her spirits had improved. She managed to smile a little and even say a few words.

Liz took her bath in the pub's best room. She couldn't walk to it. Greville had to carry her. Father Jack, who seemed to be supplied with an amazing variety of goods, had given her a bar of soap and a bottle of baby cream. Then, while Liz tried to take the aches out of her body, the rest of them settled down to their late lunch. Occasionally one of the girls would take her some more hot water, and they even tried to get her to have some food. But Liz was not hungry.

Lunch consisted of cold chicken and warm champagne. The chicken had come from the Convent of the Sacred Heart: the champagne had come from a doctor's house in Bayswater. Four bottles had been wrapped in rags and hidden in the cellar under a pile of coal and junk. But Father Jack was an indefatigable scrounger. When he searched a house he searched it thoroughly.

"Try her with some of the champers," said Father Jack, regarding the small heap of chicken bones in front of him with some satisfaction. "It can't do any harm." He grinned. "Tell her I blessed it."

There was still some left in the second bottle they had opened. Greville took it in to Liz. She had rubbed soap all over her body in a desperate and futile attempt to reduce the bruises and teeth-marks. But the heat of the water only served to accentuate them.

Greville thought it would do no harm to try a light-hearted touch. "I hope it isn't catching," he said. "You look as if you've suddenly developed measles or something all round your breasts and shoulders."

Surprisingly, Liz giggled. "It's not a disease, it's an allergy," she retorted. "My doctor warned me it was likely to develop if I had any intimate contact with members of the opposite sex."

"Father Jack has sent you some holy water. You're supposed to drink it and say to yourself: 'Whatever happens to me is for the best in this best of all possible worlds'."

"You know," said Liz, taking the bottle, "there are times when I could almost believe that—like now." She set the champagne bottle to her lips and drank greedily.

In one long draught, Greville noted with satisfaction, she drank nearly half a pint.

Liz hiccupped. "It's a lovely feeling," she said, "when it's all over. It's like when you stop banging your head on the wall. It's like waking up from a bad dream. You can see the sunlight, and you know it wasn't for real, after all."

"You were thirsty," said Greville, eyeing the empty bottle. "I'll get you some more."

"No, stay with me. Getting tight isn't the answer ... I'm all right, really, you know. I'm quite used to that sort of thing, but it's usually less strenuous ... I've wasted enough time in here. You can help me get out." She giggled again. "Then you can put some of that baby cream between my legs. I don't think I can bend far enough myself."

Greville dried her, then he applied the baby lotion. Then he helped her to dress. While he was putting her shoes and socks on, they heard the sound of a car starting. Greville dashed out of the pub just in time to see the Land Rover pulling away. One of the girls in the back waved cheerily to him, then the car picked up speed, carving a smooth double track through dandelions, foxgloves and the long high nettles of midsummer.

Greville stood there for a few moments, scratching his head and feeling perplexed and watching the Land Rover dwindling in the distance. The sound died: and then there was nothing but the sky and fields that had grown wild as the prairie and were rippling like a green inland sea under the light touch of a breeze.

Liz hobbled out of the pub. "See. I'm O.K. for walking ... What happened?"

"Father Jack took off," said Greville. "He seems to be in a hell of a hurry."

When they went to the station wagon, they found one possible reason for Father Jack's hurried departure. It had been stripped of everything—all the goods that

Greville had scrounged in London, and the rifles and ammunition that he had taken from the late Nibs and his confederates—everything except two shot-guns and twenty cartridges.

On the driver's seat there was a slip of paper on which had been scribbled a short message:

*For services rendered: I'm sure you wouldn't have objected, but why risk disagreement? Kindest regards to your good lady. The Lord will provide.*

Greville felt simultaneously extremely foolish and extremely angry. But Liz began to laugh.

"Christ!" she said helplessly. "Never trust the clergy ... You know what, Greville? I think he's my kind of transie."

And suddenly Greville was laughing, too.

## TEN

THE delay caused by the encounter with the late Nibs and his companions together with the extra time needed to give Liz her bath made it impossible for Greville to get back to Ambergreave Lake and his cottage on the island before it was dark. After they had both recovered from Father Jack's rapid departure, Greville made Liz comfortable in the station wagon, settled himself in the driver's seat and started the engine.

"No more stops," he said grimly. "Not for anyone or anything."

"What if someone else has the same idea as those other clever little bastards?"

"We don't stop. We drive round it or through it. If we can't do either, we've had it anyway. A couple of shot-guns aren't much of an arsenal." He started the car, took a last vague glance at *The Angler's Rest*, and then set off in the tracks that had been carved by Father Jack's Land Rover along the weed-covered road. He thought that if he put his foot down he stood a very good chance of overtaking the Land Rover before long. But he had no desire to overtake it. Whatever Father Jack had taken, he had earned.

So Greville let the station wagon roll along at a reasonable pace, profoundly thankful that he and Liz were still alive. After a time, he was pleased to see that Liz was dozing. She lay huddled in her seat like a small child tired out after a big party.

Some party! thought Greville. It had been hilarious. He began to sweat as he recalled how near they had both been to a particularly stupid—and sordid—form of death. But then, he reflected, all death was sordid. You could die of cancer, accidents, old age, overeating, alcoholism (if you were lucky), hunger, appendicitis, rats, cats, dogs, disease and bullets. Whatever it was, it was stupid and sordid—about as stupid and sordid as staying alive.

The road slipped by. The sun began to sink low towards the western edge of the world. The station wagon passed unmolested through small, ribbon-like villages. Greville was past caring about precautions. He had been near enough to total disaster not to worry too much about what might happen next. Goddammit, if anything was going to happen it bloody well would! So why frighten hell out of one's self by worrying about it. *Que sera, sera . . .*

Presently Liz woke.

"I'm sorry," she said.

"Don't be. A bit of rest was what you needed."

"Not about that. About landing you with me. I'm more trouble than I'm worth. If I hadn't wanted to see the Festival Hall and the British Museum everything might still have gone all right for you."

"If you hadn't got yourself into a mess on Chelsea Bridge," pointed out Greville drily, "the day might have been a hell of a lot duller. On the other hand, I might be dead by now. Who the devil knows?"

"Nevertheless," said Liz, stretching herself and wincing, "I want you to know that I'm sorry."

"Your sorrow is noted." He smiled. "It will probably be held against you."

"Where are we?"

"About forty miles from salvation. There are a few more villages to get through and a small town called Thetford. If we survive those, we stand a reasonable chance of living till morning."

"I don't even know whether I want to live till morning."

"You do. That's the trouble. We all bloody well do. It's part of the old genetic programming. When God created the world he filled it full of cretins and said: 'Now look, chaps, the great thing is not to write great poetry, create symphonies or produce paintings that make people want to cry. The great thing is to live till morning. And if you are still alive when morning comes, why then you must do your best to increase the odds against some other poor bastard. For if you don't do unto him, as sure as I knocked together this old firmament out of nothing he'll do his damndest to do unto you.' "

Liz began to laugh. "Greville," she said, "I think you're practically the greatest. You pinched me from the dogs, you lick somebody's shoes to give me a chance of living, you put baby lotion on my legs—and lose half your possessions while you're doing it—and you still let me ride in your car and try to keep me happy. You realise you're destroying my faith in human nature?"

"That is the aim," retorted Greville. "Essentially, I'm a sadist."

The sun slipped smoothly over the horizon. The twilight that followed was hardly light enough to drive by, but it suited Greville's programme. He did not switch the car's headlamps on. Instead he dropped speed to little more than twenty miles an hour and stayed in third gear. He was hoping to slip through Thetford—the last real danger point before Ambergreave—in as inconspicuous a manner as possible.

By the time they reached the outskirts of the town stars were pricking the now turquoise eggshell of the sky. Greville's eyes were tired with peering through the windscreen; but they were not too tired to notice the flickering of an oil lamp about a hundred yards along the road.

It was a typical night prowlers' set-up, he thought. Someone would be listening for cars, someone else would be organising the block and, no doubt, a small posse of transnormal citizenry would be ready to pounce if they thought the attack could be carried through without much loss.

"Poke a shot-gun through the side window," said Greville. 'Don't shoot until I tell you, and don't shoot at anything but lights."

At the same time as they swung the searchlight on him, Greville switched on his own headlamps. The road block was a poor one—it was only a farm trailer. Furthermore, there was a wide grass verge on the right; and if he drove straight at the three men who were standing on it in the glare of his headlamps, he stood a good chance of getting through.

"Now!" he shouted.

The first barrel accomplished nothing except a vaguely human scream; but Liz had better luck with her second try. The searchlight went out.

Greville put his foot down and headed straight for the three men. They began shooting, but the car's headlamps must have ruined their aim. The station wagon lurched sickeningly as it hit the grass verge. Then there was a heavy thud and a bump as it hit at least one of them. Then it was through.

For good measure, Liz fired a couple of backward parting shots, but they probably accomplished nothing. For now there was only darkness once more. Greville switched his lights off immediately, and almost by instinct found his way back to the road.

"Not long, now," he said. "Providing we get through the town in one piece. Things aren't quite tough enough yet in this part of the world to make people really desperate. The great danger is not from the locals but from nomads."

"That road block seemed like a local affair," observed Liz.

"It was. But they weren't really trying, and they hadn't had much experience. Otherwise we wouldn't be here."

Liz yawned. "You almost fill me with optimism."

He laughed grimly. "Sometimes I even convince myself."

They passed through Thetford without any more difficulty. Greville was on home territory and knew his way sufficiently to take the narrow streets at a speed high enough to dismiss all danger of spontaneous attacks. The only thing to be feared was a well prepared block; but fortunately they didn't encounter any.

When they were clear of the town, he switched on his headlamps once more, and Liz saw that the car was running along a smooth straight road flanked on either side by tall trees.

"Thetford Chase," said Greville. "It used to be a national park or something like that. Plenty of deer. I'll bring you hunting some time."

"Cheers for the rustic life."

"It has its moments."

A few minutes later they came to the village of Ambergreave. Greville gave a long blast on the car's horn. It startled Liz out of a semi-doze.

"What the hell did you do that for?"

"A local signal," explained Greville. "No sense in running the risk of collecting unnecessary pot-shots. Just possibly somebody might be tempted."

Liz was surprised. "You mean they won't attack just because you live round here?"

"It's not an infallible rule. But as I told you, we're not entirely down to cannibalism in these parts yet."

Ambergreave was a long straggly village with most of the houses and cottages set well apart. It took longer to drive through than the town of Thetford and it seemed totally deserted. Presently the station wagon turned off the hard road. Greville changed down into second gear, nursing the car along a narrow bumpy track. Presently the track widened then sloped gently down to the edge of Ambergreave Lake, a broad expanse of water, still as a mirror, reflecting the large low moon like an orange lantern.

Greville drove along the edge of the lake to a small jetty, then pulled the car up and switched off the engine. But he left the headlamps on, and Liz saw that they were illuminating the shape of a small rowing dinghy.

She got out of the car, stretched herself cautiously and watched Greville go down to the boat. He lay down on his stomach on the jetty and put his arms into the water, evidently feeling for something round the side of the dinghy.

"What are you doing?"

"De-fusing the transport," he retorted laconically.

Presently he stood up and held out his hands towards

her. There was a grenade in each, with a long trailing piece of wire linking them both.

"If anyone wants to come visiting," he explained, "they have to use the boat. In which case they blow themselves to glory."

Liz gazed across the stretch of water at the vaguely outlined patch of land on which Greville's cottage stood.

"How nice to live on an island," she said.

"Don't we all?" said Greville. "There was once a character called John Donne who used to write poetry and think otherwise. But he was a nut-case. A real nut-case. He had delusions of grandeur ... Yes, poor old Donne was up the spout—a regular transie." He stowed the grenades in the car, switched off the headlamps and locked the doors. "The trouble is, everybody lives on islands and nobody knows how to build rowing-boats ... Now come and sit at the back here, and I'll ferry you home—just like they used to do in the romantic movies."

Liz stepped into the boat and sat down. "It would be nice to be able to go to the pictures," she said wistfully.

Greville took the oars and pushed off. Suddenly he began to laugh.

"What's so funny?"

"It's just occurred to me," said Greville, "that at least ninety per cent of all the film-stars must have survived—for a time at least. Which just goes to show that God—if there is a god—must have a nice sense of humour."

## ELEVEN

On the outside and by moonlight Greville's retreat looked like an uneasy hybrid of miniature pagan temple and Victorian public convenience. It had a broad flight of steps leading up to a small portico flanked by Lilliputian marble columns. The whole of its front was faced with large blocks of some kind of stone; but, as Liz later discovered, the sides and back were of Suffolk brick and with ordinary cottage windows. The steeply sloping roof was covered with pantiles, adding a vague suggestion of the Japanese to its mixed ancestry.

Greville tied up the dinghy and led Liz up the steps to the massive double-front door—a thing of oak and studs and wrought iron. He pushed it open, felt on the inside wall and pressed a switch. An electric light came on, and somewhere there was the subdued noise of a generator starting automatically.

"It's marvellous," said Liz, surveying the electric light and the untidy but comfortable room that it illuminated.

"It's what happens when an English country gentleman gets an acropolis complex with pagoda complications," remarked Greville drily. "Let's get to bed for Christ's sake. It's been somewhat of a day ... Do you want anything to eat first?"

"All I want," said Liz, "is unconsciousness."

"You can have that for free."

The bedroom was a small poky room leading off the far end of the living room. It looked like an afterthought—as indeed it was, along with the tiny kitchen. It contained nothing but a large bed, a chest of drawers and a thick rug that lent a touch of luxury and decadence to the dull brick floor.

"If you want to pee or have a shit," said Greville, "you'll have to go outside. There's a lavatory of sorts just through the kitchen door."

"I don't want to do anything," yawned Liz, "except sleep. I've just about had my lot for today ... Are we sleeping together?"

"There's only one bed," Greville pointed out. "If you prefer the floor you can have it."

"I don't, but on the other hand I don't think I could face a good screw tonight ... Not," she hastened to add, "that I'm suggesting anything. It's just that I'm still sore enough not to want it."

"You disappoint me," said Greville. "I was just getting myself in the mood for an all-night sex orgy. Now shut up and get into bed."

He went out of the bedroom and bolted the outer door, then he came back and bolted the bedroom door. Liz took off her few clothes. So did Greville. He did not look at her.

"Get into bed. I'll switch off the light."

She got into bed and waited for him. Greville kicked off his shoes, switched out the light and joined her. There was a sudden silence as the generator ceased producing electricity.

For a while they lay side by side, not touching, each of them naked and each of them conscious of the other's nearness. The darkness and the silence were absolute. They were two children alone in the cosmos, with no one to comfort them but each other.

Greville, tired though he was, found that he could not sleep. So did Liz. They were too close to each other for comfort—too close and yet too far away.

"Greville," whispered Liz at last, "if you want it, I think I can face it."

"Shut up and go to sleep. I don't want any damn thing."

Liz smiled in the darkness. "Everybody wants something. If they didn't they'd just die ... What do you want?"

"Peace," said Greville.

"You can't get it alone."

"How do you know?"

"I've tried. If I thought I could get it alone I wouldn't have worried about Jane."

"I don't give a tinker's cuss for Jane."

'I know."

'I don't give a tinker's cuss for you, either."

"Liar! Not for me as a person, maybe. But you want me to depend on you."

"Don't be stupid. You are just a bloody complication."

Liz rolled herself against him. "I expect that's what you need. I bet you've been looking for a bloody complication for quite a while."

In the darkness Greville hit her. "You're madder than most," he said heavily. "You like to press your luck."

Her face stung, but Liz didn't turn away. The tears trickled silently down her cheek, and she kept her voice steady so that Greville would not know about them.

"So I'm right, then," she murmured. "Does it frighten you that somebody else knows?"

Greville hit her again. "Now shut up and go to sleep. Remember you can't dial 999 any more. I can do what the hell I like with you."

"Good night," said Liz.

"Good night."

Neither of them slept. For an hour or more, Greville tossed and turned, trying, as he thought, to find a comfortable position. Liz just lay there in the dark, wide-eyed and waiting.

Presently, he grabbed hold of her roughly. There were no preliminaries. "Serves you right, doesn't it?" he shouted. "All you want to do is be flat on your back with your legs wide open."

But he had to turn her on her back and open her legs himself.

Liz said nothing. There was nothing to say. Besides, it was very painful and she felt that if she used her voice at all she would scream or cry out.

Mercifully, Greville didn't take long to reach a climax. And when he had finished, when his body became slack and relaxed, when Liz knew that she had conquered the impulse to scream, she cradled him, holding his head to her breast as if he were a small child. She soothed him and whispered meaningless words to him. And so they lay together—each feeling tired and lonely and lost—until daybreak.

## TWELVE

THE day was a most unusual one: it rained from before dawn till after dusk. Greville found later that he could not recall whether it was months or years ago when it had last rained all day. He lay on his back in bed with Liz at his side—doubtless pretending to be asleep—and gazed in delight at the raindrops running down the grey dawn window.

He concentrated and tried to remember what he had been doing during the last downpour. The memory wouldn't come, and because it wouldn't come it annoyed him. It continued to annoy him throughout the rest of the day; for as the rain showed no signs of ceasing, he realised that it was a rather special occasion. There must have been other similar occasions, but they were lost in the fuzz of transnormal happenings in a wholly transnormal world. It was the fact that he couldn't remember the last time it rained all day that caused him, in the end, to start a diary.

But meanwhile he lay in bed and watched the rain make patterns on the window, and wondered for perhaps the ten thousandth time why he was still alive.

He looked at Liz and saw her face in the grey light—a face without cares or wrinkles, frozen by time. The face of a child. A dead child ... There was something in him that wanted to cry ...

Liz stirred. The child was resurrected as a woman.

"I'm sorry about last night," he said. "It must have hurt you."

"Not much. Besides, I belong to you for the time being. You can do what you like, can't you?" The words were hard but the voice was soft. Liz felt she was only stating the fact.

But the statement triggered off an internal explosion for Greville. "Nobody belongs to anybody," he snapped. "And especially you don't belong to me. Now if you can divest yourself of the puppy mentality, we'll get up and see about breakfast."

Liz was not perturbed. "What's that scar on your stomach?"

"An old bayonet wound. The only way I could get out of a coal mine was to play dead. Somebody prodded me just to make sure. It didn't work ... Now, breakfast."

Breakfast was a lavish affair. Greville managed to produce ham, eggs and home-made bread. He even had a bottle of coffee extract.

Liz was delighted. "Where did you get all this stuff."

"I have connections," he said briefly. "I told you things weren't too hard yet in this part of the world."

Much to his surprise the rain was still coming down when breakfast was over.

"What would you like to do today?" he asked.

"Nothing much."

"That suits me fine. There are one or two things I

have to do, but they won't take long. While I'm doing them, you can tidy this place up."

He put on oil-skins and went out into the rain to feed the half-dozen hens that he had caught and partially tamed. When he had done that, he poured some petrol with miserly care into the fuel tank of his petrol-paraffin powered generator. Then he topped up the car batteries that provided his illumination. By the time he got back to the folly, the bed was made and the pots had been washed. Liz had found out how to work the two-stroke pump in the kitchen.

"Go easy with the detergent," warned Greville, noticing the legacy of suds in the sink. "That is one of the things that is very hard to come by."

The rain continued, and he didn't know what to do. If he had been by himself the answer would have been simple. He would have settled down with a book and would probably have lost himself in it till hunger called. Greville was a great one for books. Other people's books. Books he would like to have written himself. He read them with enthusiasm, delight, disgust, guilt, ecstasy, impatience and envy. But whether they were good, bad or indifferent he always read them with envy. For they were the children that he had never had.

Chiefly he read novels—stories of a world that no longer existed and that almost seemed now as if it could never have existed. His favourite dislike was an old-fashioned novel called *Room At The Top*. He felt somehow that it was a kind of photographic negative of certain aspects of his own early life. A negative because, basically, he had never wanted to occupy room at the top. But Pauline had wanted it, and so he had masqueraded for a while as an ambitious go-getter.

Greville collected and hoarded books the way some transies still collected and hoarded money. Neither were going to be much use, he thought, in a transnormal world. But the compulsion was obsessional. Besides, books were almost as good as brandy. They provided an avenue of escape, and the hangover was less noticeable. Also they were considerably easier to come by than brandy. Pretty soon the supply of brandy would give out. But the supply of books would last for a long time yet. Only the rats ate them; and although they were good for lighting fires they were not satisfactory as a basic fuel . . .

Greville was tempted to ignore Liz, settle himself with a book, and treat her as if she didn't exist. The only flaw in the proposition was the last bit. He couldn't treat her as if she didn't exist. He had lived alone too long not to be acutely and painfully conscious of someone else's presence. Besides, he had virtually added to her quota of the previous day's rapes.

"I'd better show you where things are," he said at length. "Then you won't need to keep running to me for every little thing you want."

Liz had already discovered the larder, which was surprisingly well stocked with tinned food, bacon, eggs and even fresh butter. Greville took her into the living-room, threw back a rug, and lifted a trap-door.

"The wine cellar of one, Augustus Rowley, visionary, philosopher and man of letters," he announced.

Liz laughed. "Who died of languishment and a profound melancholy."

Greville was surprised. "Who told you that?"

"You did—yesterday morning when we were having breakfast by Cleopatra's Needle . . . It's funny. It already seems about a year ago."

Oddly Greville didn't remember. But he was pleased that she had remembered. "Time is subjective," he announced drily. "I thought you would have defined it as several screws ago."

"I thought you didn't like me to talk about screwing."

"*Touché*. Now come and see what the cellar holds."

The cellar held an incongruous store of goods that Greville had collected patiently and sometimes at great risk over a long period. There were piles of canned goods—mostly soup, vegetables and fruit. But there were also some tins of corned beef.

And there were two .45 revolvers, a small .38 and an ancient .303 rifle together with boxes of ammunition. There were also several hand-grenades and a stack of perhaps thirty five-gallon cans of petrol together with a very large drum of paraffin. There were also trousers and jackets of varying shapes and sizes, shirts, shoes, socks, bottles of beer, wine and spirits, rat traps, a tin of strychnine, a small astronomical telescope, reels of cotton, balls of wool, a few bales of printed cloth, more books, a first-aid kit and a bottle of choloroform, a sack of potatoes (some of which were sprouting), two violins, a box of soap tablets and a few tins of cigarettes.

"It's wonderful," breathed Liz, surveying the treasures. "You must have had a hard job getting this lot together."

"The squirrel mentality," said Greville. "You won't believe it, but the only thing I had to shoot anybody for was the telescope. I took it from what was left of a junk-shop in Norwich. An old man saw me and started popping off with a shot-gun. I couldn't get out of the place unless I shot back. He peppered me and it hurt so much and I got so mad that I damn near blew his head off . . . People die for the oddest things, you know. And the joke is I didn't really want the telescope anyway. It was just something to carry."

"Have you ever used it?" she asked.

"No."

"Then we shall use it some night when the sky is clear. And you'll set it up and I can look at the moon."

"What the hell for?"

"To give an old man in Norwich a reason for dying," she said simply.

It did not take long to complete the tour of inspection of Greville's cottage. Liz looked at his books and at his large collection of records and at the twelve-volt record player that had been a major prize of an early scrounging expedition.

"Will it really work?" she asked, fingering it in obvious delight.

"Try it and see."

Liz chose a Strauss record—the Emperor Waltz—and the music seemed to fill the cottage, briefly shutting out time, transnormality and all the bitter memories of recent years. After the Strauss she tried another record, a song, this time, which she remembered having heard as a child. The name of the singer, Marlene Dietrich, meant nothing to Liz; but the song, *Where Have All The Flowers Gone*, brought tears to her eyes.

Greville remained unmoved—or gave the appearance of remaining unmoved. He did not want Liz to think that he was a push-over for such sentimental nonsense.

The morning wore on. They both became hungry. Because it was too wet to go out shooting and because there was no fresh meat or vegetables in the larder, Greville permitted himself the luxury of opening cans.

For lunch they had soup and baked beans and pineapple. And because it was somehow a special sort of day, Greville went really reckless and opened one of his three remaining bottles of *Asti Spumante*.

The wine relaxed them. Greville yawned and looked through the window at the low grey sky and the smooth curtain of rain. It fascinated him.

'A raindrop,' he said suddenly and disconcertingly, "is like a glass cathedral. It's a place for worship. One ought to be small enough to walk inside and drown in liquid prayer."

"Raindrops fall," Liz pointed out. "They get destroyed."

Greville hiccupped and shook his head. "They change, that's all. Then somehow or other they get back to the ocean and back again into the sky ... Perpetual motion ... Perpetual prayer ... Let's go to bed. I'm tired."

A flicker of apprehension passed over Liz's face. She was remembering the soreness between her legs, and she was also remembering the previous night.

Greville laughed. "Not for that," he said. "Enough is as good as a feast. We'll be chaste little children taking our after-lunch naps. Hell, what else is there to do? We can't bloody well go out and save the world."

"I'll clear the table first," said Liz.

"You'll come to bed. Suburban efficiency doesn't suit you."

"Do I strip?"

"Do what the hell you like. I'm stripping. I feel better that way."

"Can we listen to some music?"

"No. I want to sleep."

"Oh, well," said Liz, eyeing the record player. "I suppose there's plenty of time."

Greville pretended to be irritated. "Put some bloody music on, then, if that's what you want. But turn the volume down."

Liz looked through the records as she took off her clothes. She found the Italian Symphony and put it on.

Then she went into the bedroom. Greville had already closed his eyes. But when she got into bed he put his hand on her breast and let it lie there lightly.

"Maybe it's as well I didn't let the dogs have you," he murmured drowsily. "Just possibly you might teach me how to become human."

Liz said nothing. She was lost in the strangely sad gaiety of Mendelssohn. She didn't so much listen to the music as inhale it, each breath drawing her deeper into a sea of unbeing with the insistence of an anaesthetic.

She was asleep long before the record ended. So was Greville. Despite the rain and the proximity of each other, they both slept profoundly. Greville was the first to wake, by which time it was already growing dark. He looked at Liz in the dim light and was suddenly and unaccountably afraid. He wanted to kill her or run away from her—or both. His hand was still on her breast; but the impulse to let it slide up and fasten tightly round her neck was sudden and fierce.

He tried to control it and couldn't.

Of its own volition, apparently, the hand started to move.

Liz woke. She looked at him. The hand had already reached her neck.

"It doesn't matter," she said softly. "You can do what you like." There was no fear in her voice.

Greville laughed shakily. The spell was broken. "It's still raining," he said. "Damned if I can remember when it last rained as long as this . . . Let's get up."

## THIRTEEN

The first entry in Greville's diary was written late that evening when the rain had stopped and when Liz, having satiated herself with an orgy of music, was indulging in such domestic activities as remaking the bed and clearing away the remains of a late meal. The diary itself was an old school exercise book that Greville had found in a deserted cottage. The uneven and faded writing on the cover proclaimed it to be the English Book of one

Robert Andrew Cherry, age 11. Robert Andrew Cherry, who was doubtless long since dead, had also obligingly supplied the date on which he had received his English Book: April 30th, 1972.

Whatever had happened to the boy must have happened soon afterwards for he had only managed to do three short pieces of work. One of these was an essay entitled *What I want to be when I grow up.* It was the essay that had made Greville want to keep the book.

"When I grow up," Robert Cherry had written, "I want to be a man who writes stories. I would write good stories. I would not write children's stories. I would write stories that would be read by lots of grown-ups. Then I would be famous. I would have a red car and a big house and my wife would be very proud because I was famous. I would write stories about spaceships and distant planets. Some of my stories would be made into films. Then I would be rich and would not have to work any more. I would let my father live with me and look after the garden. Then he would be too busy to be unhappy because my mother is dead. I would give my father a red car, too, but he cannot drive."

Greville had kept the book because Robert Cherry, doubtless a victim—direct or indirect—of the Radiant Suicide, was also the ghost of Greville's own childhood. That was how it had once been . . .

Now the unused pages of Robert Cherry's English Book were to be put to use at last. Greville considered tearing out the essay and the two spelling exercises that followed it. Then he decided against it. Instead he turned the book upside down so that it was back to front.

He found a pencil and, after a few moments' thought, he wrote at the top of the pages: "For Robert—who would have known better."

Then he made the first entry:

"July 8th, 1981 (give or take a little). Day Two for certain. Yesterday I kept a rendezvous—dead drunk—with Pauline on Chelsea Bridge. I also cheated the dogs of a breakfast called Liz.

"The girl is good for nothing, as she puts it, but screwing. And she's had plenty of that. But somehow she's still oddly innocent. She wants to go looking for a twin sister; and I have an idea that I'll do my damnedest to stop her ... What was it that overrated poet once said? 'Teach us to care and not to care. Teach us to sit still'.

"I don't know about sitting still, but I'd like to have the first bit. Last night I 'screwed' Liz—the first in a long time. Tonight I almost killed her. Liz has life, and maybe I'm envious of life. Whatever happens to her there's always the cheap little consolation that but for me she would have been dead anyway ...

"It's been raining all day. I can't remember when it last rained all day. And because of that I have a crazy thought at the back of my mind that history is being lost. My history. The rain has made me realise that I still have the greatest vanity. I don't want my history to be lost. This is my bid for immortality—by courtesy of the rain and Robert Cherry. And so to bed."

But Greville didn't immediately go to bed. The rain had stopped, the sky had cleared and Liz had finished her work. She wanted to go out for a breath of air. So he took her round the tiny island. And they gazed at the lake and the faint patina of stars in a high washed sky. And before they came back to the cottage he kissed her. He had screwed her already. Already he had wanted to kill her. But this was the first time he had kissed her. He was surprised to find that, oddly, it hurt like a knife.

They went to bed chastely and lay close together with an oddly impersonal tenderness. For a time they made desultory conversation in subdued voices, almost as if they were afraid of being overheard. Greville had been troubled by that kiss. He was still troubled—so, experimentally, he tried again. And again it hurt.

It was not so much a pain as a terrible tightness. The tightness started in his chest and seemed to wind round his body until his breathing became shallow and he could feel a faint dampness of perspiration on his head. In the darkness his thoughts began to turn to Pauline. He did not want to think of Pauline. But the struggle was a hard and conscious one; and the tightness spread from his body into the muscles of his legs and arms.

Liz was aware of his tension but she did not remark upon it. She had been with many men who had betrayed their stresses in various ways. She prided herself on being able to take things as they came; and for the time being she had found comfort, security and companionship. There was, she felt, nothing more that one could hope for—except that whenever death came, as it inevitably would, it would be a quick and easy one.

Presently, still holding each other, they each fell into an uneasy sleep. Liz had nightmares, and once she woke up screaming. She dreamt that she was in a cage, naked, in a large and rather foul-smelling room. She dreamt that tit-bits of food were being thrown to her between the bars and that she was given a bowl from which to drink. But when she drank the liquid burned her throat. Presently the door opened and men came into the cage. They were large and coarse and hot with lust. They began to do things to her, and the dreadful thing was that she could not struggle. And the even more dreadful thing was that she began to like it. She hated the foul breath, the grunts, the weight, the sudden spasms of pain. She hated the way her limbs were responding, the way her mouth opened, the way her breasts began to work against her like independent sabateurs. She loathed the whole horrible situation; but somehow she did not want it to end.

And it was the feeling that there were forces making her like what she hated, that caused her to scream.

Greville shook her and slapped her. The screams dissolved into moans, and the moans became translated into an uncontrollable sobbing. Presently she felt exhausted and empty. Presently she slept once more—with Greville holding her so tight that his arms began to ache. Morning was a long time coming.

When it came, it was as if—apart from a lingering freshness, the deluge of the previous day might never have been. The sun rose into a clear blue sky. And Day Three, as Greville later recorded in his diary, was the happiest time he had ever known in his life. Despite the years of transnormality and hardship, despite the multi-megadeath of normal man, despite the recent excursion into a London of the dead and dying, despite homicidal teenagers, humiliation and ambush, Greville felt as if he did not have a care in the world.

After breakfast—and, as he told himself, simply to cheer Liz up—he proposed a picnic. A further extravagant onslaught was made on the wine and tinned goods. Then they rowed ashore while the sun was still low in the sky, and Greville showed Liz the churchyard where Augustus Rowley was buried.

Together they read the inscription below the marble statue:

*To the undying memory of Augustus Rowley, visionary, philosopher and man of letters. Born 1833: died 1873 of languishment and a profound melancholy. He here awaits the vindication of time and circumstance, secure in the belief that he accurately interpreted the call of his Maker.*

Liz uncorked the wine. "To Augustus Rowley, guardian and patron saint of all good transies." She drank from the bottle and handed it to Greville.

"To Augustus," he said, "without whose vision and philosophy two transies at least would have been considerably the poorer."

They spent the whole day in the churchyard. They read some more epitaphs and then made love in the long grasses of high summer between a tablet commemorating the interment of Abigail Sarah Busterd, gathered unto her Lord in 1909, and James Jolly, called from on high in 1923.

Afterwards they slept peacefully and tranquilly though Greville's hand remained at all times on his shot-gun. Then they woke, read some more epitaphs and drank some more wine. They were not disturbed, and in the heat of the afternoon they bathed in the hypnotic glare of the sun and talked happily and freely of a world that each of them found difficult to remember. Finally, and as if to celebrate the continued absence of disaster, they made love yet again in the late afternoon before making their way back to the lake and its island citadel.

It was a golden day. They saw no one. They were threatened by no predators, human or animal. They could have been alone in the country in an entirely normal world—except that there were no planes to cut the blue sky into slices with their vapour trails and penetrating wedges of noise. Nor were there any cars to transform the weed-covered roads into battlegrounds. Nor were there any sane specimens of officialdom to object to the joyful and carefree desecration of holy ground.

Before they left the churchyard, Liz made a garland of buttercups and daisies to hang round the marble neck of Augustus Rowley; and Greville carefully balanced the empty wine bottle on the surprisingly flat top of the statue's head.

## FOURTEEN

THE weather remained fine. The days blended gently into each other. July seemed to have expended its total rainfall in that single downpour. Optimistically, Greville began to think that Liz would eventually lose the silly notion of going off into the deep blue yonder to look for her twin sister. But he reckoned without the nightmares. They came fairly frequently—about every two or three days.

The girl in the cage, Liz had explained to him in a matter-of-fact way, was not really herself but Jane. Somewhere, the northerners who had stolen her from the Richmond Lot were keeping Jane and treating her on the level of an animal—an animal that was useful for entertainment only. Greville neither believed nor disbelieved in telepathy or telepathic dreams; but he displayed strong scepticism simply in order to counter the sudden fits of restlessness and depression that Liz began to experience. He had found a kind of contentment and a kind of satisfaction that he had not thought could exist. It would come to an end, as all things would come to an end, but he wanted it to last as long as possible.

Liz was a mass of conflicts. She was becoming accustomed to Greville. He treated her far better than she had been treated in Richmond; and she was beginning to learn how to deal with his black moods. But there was still the pull of Jane. And there were the nightmares, when, in effect and for a briefly horrible time, she *became* Jane, experiencing her degradation and the hopelessness of her plight.

Greville began to devise distractions. There were only ten or twelve people still living in the village of Ambergreave, and only two who were actually dangerous. The rest, by unspoken and common consent, seemed to live on a *laissez-faire* basis—recognising still a basic pattern of interdependence that the disintegration of society had not wholly destroyed. Greville introduced Liz to the few people with whom he had any dealings and taught her to avoid the cottage where Big Willie Crutchley lived incestuously with his mother and on principle attempted to kill almost anything that moved.

Big Willie was half-idiot and half-genius. Half-idiot because he only wanted to destroy, and half-genius because he had adapted almost perfectly to the new conditions. Realising that eventually there would be an end to guns and ammunition, Big Willie had taught himself to survive independent of them. He reverted to the primitive approach. For hunting and for personal defence he became expert in the use of sling and cross-bow—both devised and manufactured by himself without reference to humanity's previous experience, for Big Willie could neither read nor write. In the old days he had been inferior; but ten years of Omega radiation had placed him among the surviving élite. For large semi-wild animals such as deer, pigs and bulls, he dug pits and planted sharpened stakes in them. For small creatures such as dogs and cats he devised cunning snares.

Big Willie and his mother would eat anything—including, so it was said, human beings. But they, too, at least partially accepted the principle of *laissez-faire* for they had never been known to eat anyone who lived in Ambergreave. And he only fired warning shafts from his crossbow if anybody was so careless as to come too near his pits and traps. Of course, if the warning shafts were ignored . . .

Big Willie and Greville conscientiously avoided crossing each other's path. Greville realised that Big Willie was probably waiting until he ran out of ammunition. But, Greville promised himself, when that time drew close, he would remember to deal with Big Willie first.

Perhaps the most useful and most efficient member of the small community—if it could be so described—was Miss Worrall.

Miss Worrall lived in a derelict windmill. At least the windmill, an old tower mill, had been derelict for half a century until Miss Worrall installed herself. That was in the early days of the Radiant Suicide before normal man realised that his number was up. Miss Worrall was an ex-music teacher of indeterminate age who had developed a passion for dogs and the simple life.

She came to Ambergreave with two Alsatians, and she adopted the derelict mill as her home. The Alsatians multiplied, and were very carefully and strictly trained. At the same time, Miss Worrall (no one ever discovered her Christian name) perhaps with a flash of insight or clairvoyance, began to renovate the windmill. The surviving villagers claimed it was impossible; there were those who could remember the 1914 war but could not remember the tower mill ever having sails. Nevertheless, Miss Worrall constructed sails, doing all the carpentering herself and only soliciting help to get the new sails into position. Then she found a mason who still retained enough skill to fashion a tolerable pair of millstones—and, lo, the windmill was a going concern once more.

Miss Worrall began to grind corn. As the years of Omega radiation wrought havoc with the outside world, she continued to grind corn; and, for a time, her business throve as all the powered mechanical mills came to a stop. But then the farms began to disintegrate, and there was less corn to grind. Prudently, Miss Worrall allowed her pack of Alsatians to increase to eight. Once, and because it was known that she always kept a good supply of flour, the mill was attacked by a dozen or so armed, determined and hungry men. They did not get any flour; and several of them had their throats torn out by the Alsatians. Since then, Miss Worrall had lived in peace. There was still a little wheat to grind, for the surviving villagers grew patches of it here and there; and Miss Worrall never took more than a tenth of the harvest for her services. She lived alone with her dogs, an old piano and about twenty faded photographs of the same man. Greville liked her. He had good reason to; for she had once saved him when he was starving.

So he introduced Liz to Miss Worrall, and he introduced her to the Cuthbert family—Charles Cuthbert, a large florid man with two wives and two half-grown children, was the local blacksmith and machine fixer—and to Alaric Newton, R.A., who lived in a tree house and painted in oils and had once been one of the best marksmen with a rifle in England.

Liz got on well with Miss Worrall and would occasionally pay a social visit on her own. Presently she had almost the same degree of control over the Alsatians as their owner.

Now and then Greville would take Liz hunting with him. It was not necessary to travel far to go hunting for, with the exception of a few small patches of land close to the villages, the countryside had reverted to a degree of wildness that was surprising in view of the fact that it was only a few years since society had relinquished its control. On these occasions Greville would arm himself with a rifle and a pistol, while Liz carried one of the shot-guns. Between them, he felt, they had quite enough fire-power to deal with everything except rats ... And possibly humans ...

Greville's favourite quarry was pig—the semi-wild and surprisingly dangerous variety that had adapted so well to the new-found freedom. Of all the domesticated creatures, the pig had done best since the passing of normal man; and, in fact the pig population of Britain now exceeded the population of transies.

The strength of the pigs lay in their ability to eat practically everything—including, if necessary, each other. Greville was rapidly becoming an expert in pigs. He could tell the carnivorous ones at a glance. And, whenever possible, he avoided them; for there was a strong and most un-piggy flavour to their flesh. They did not make good pork and they did not make good bacon. All that they were fit for was stew—and they had to be very well cooked at that.

One afternoon, when Greville and Liz were out hunting a few miles from Ambergreave, they witnessed an astounding sight. They were in a small patch of woodland, and it was one of those still summer days when sound carries tremendously and when it seems almost possible to shout and be heard from one end of the land to the other.

Having disposed of a light lunch, Greville and Liz were resting under a large and obviously ancient oak whose low leafy branches spread out to make a wide green and brown umbrella, obliterating the blue sky. Greville was half-dozing when suddenly he became aware of a faint and distant whisper. It seemed to be growing in volume. Greville had heard such a whisper before. He looked at Liz, but she was totally unconcerned and had probably not heard it.

The whisper grew, and then a new sound was added—a muffled throbbing that shook the earth and that came from a different direction. The throbbing was not so easily identifiable. It could be pigs, horses or deer.

Greville stirred uncomfortably. As the throbbing increased, the whispering seemed to disperse until it was all around them. He looked at the oak tree and then he looked at Liz.

"I think it's time to do a bit of climbing," he said. "We're going to have visitors."

Liz was getting familiar with country noises. "It's a pretty large herd—whatever they are. Sounds heavy enough for horses . . . What's the other sound?"

"If it's what I think it is," retorted Greville, "we shall very likely wish it wasn't. Come on, there's no time to waste. I'll give you a leg up."

Liz slung her shot-gun round her shoulder and began to climb the tree. Greville hauled himself after her.

The throbbing stopped, then started again, then stopped and started once more. Horses, pigs or deer—they were drawing closer. But the whispering, now much louder, seemed to be everywhere.

Greville and Liz were perched on each side of a thick forked branch about fifteen feet above the ground. Greville wedged himself into a reasonably good shooting position. He took the shot-gun from Liz and gave her the pistol. In the circumstances the shot-gun seemed likely to be their best guarantee of salvation.

From the forked branch their view of the ground below was restricted to a small irregular patch of a few square yards. This was not a great drawback, reflected Greville, for if they could not see much, neither also could they be seen.

Presently a pig passed below him. Then another and another. Although it was high summer, they had the look of very hungry carnivorous pigs. Greville was surprised. But he was less surprised when he realised how many there were, for the grunting and snorting he heard seemed to indicate that the wood was full of them.

But above and around all the pig-like noises there was the ubiquitous whispering. Even the pigs were scared. They milled to and fro as if trying to decide on a direction.

Then the first wave of rats came.

A brown tide seemed to surge over the grass and even over the squealing pigs. Suddenly there were rats everywhere. Greville had never seen so many before. At times there was the crazy illusion that the brown tide was three or four rats deep. The stench was nauseating.

The rats, evidently, had been driving the pigs and had now managed to surround them. They were coming in for the kill.

But, as victims, the carnivorous pigs were less than obliging. The rats leaped at their ears, snouts, legs, tails; and many of the pigs seemed at times to be totally covered in rats. But they careered about, trampling the rats in their hundreds. They rolled on them, snapping at them and even screamed at them. But still the rats came on.

It was a contest in which neither side could claim a decisive victory, for eventually the surviving pigs broke through the thinned-out cordon of their attackers. In the matter of escape, their speed proved decisive. Presently, there was nothing left below the oak tree but a couple of dead pigs covered totally in rats.

Liz was sick.

She clung to the oak tree for dear life, but the remains of her lunch fell steaming to the ground. The rats looked up. Bright beady eyes registered movement. Some of them began to desert the carcasses of the pigs and make for the tree-trunk.

Greville waited until a dozen or so had started to climb. Then he let them have a blast from the twelve-bore shot-gun. Most of the rats fell back dead or mortally wounded. The rest scampered away. But in a few seconds they were trying again.

It cost Greville ten cartridges—more than half the shot-gun ammunition he was carrying—before the rats gave up. Then he and Liz had to stay in their tree for half the afternoon while the surviving rats stripped the dead pigs. Eventually they moved away. Eventually there was silence

"I think it's safe for us to go down now," said Greville at length.

"Oh, God!" said Liz, white-faced and shaking. "Get me home quick, then I can have my hysterics in peace."

Greville climbed down first and scouted around to see if any of the rats were left. He did not find a single one—living. The pigs had been reduced almost to skeletons and so had the dead rats. The tide of destruction had passed, leaving behind it only the warm, foul and obscenely intimate smell of death.

As they made their way hurriedly back to the lake, Greville dwelt with silent and obscure satisfaction on the fact that Liz, in a moment of stress, had used the word "home".

## FIFTEEN

Extracts from Greville's diary:

"August. Day thirty-one, I think. Hell, I've lost track. The stars are pursuing their appointed courses, the sun is slowly burning itself to a celestial cinder, the moon still continues to go round the earth—and humanity is lying in little bits all over the planet, like the tiny parts of a vast and horribly broken clock.

"But where is the mainspring? What made us go? What was it that took us gibbering out of the trees and planted us in chromium-plated cities? What was the great sane tick-tock of civilisation all about? And why did it all explode pitifully like a home-made bomb when some fiery little pot-hole on the sun set up a ham radio station and started beaming: 'Time, gentlemen, please'?

"Christ, I can't even ask questions that are worth asking. The gods have an odd sense of humour. So I'll abolish them. There are no more gods, by order, Matthew Greville, transnormal and illiterate, hereditary custodian of one million years of evolution, great ape of the second coming . . .

"I love Liz. The thought terrifies me. I love Liz. It's a sickness. It's the sickest transnormal joke that any transie could possibly play on himself. What place is there for love in this best of all possible worlds? Love only thyself, brother, for the great day of spiritual masturbation is at hand. Love only the quick screw and the sudden violence and the sleep that sometimes passeth without dreams.

"But, sweet Christ, I love Liz—and it hurts like mad and it makes me afraid and sometimes it even gives me the illusion of no longer being alone.

"What is she? A hot little bitch who sold her body for a meal or two a day and anybody's bed at night. But let him that is without sin throw the first fit.

"My God! There are times when she's beautiful. She stands there in a torn shirt and a patched-up pair of jeans, skinning a rabbit and looking as if she could launch a thousand ships. And sometimes she lies down with nothing on at all and her legs wide open, and you'd think there was nothing to it but a sweet ten minutes of erection and demolition work.

"But suddenly the sex doesn't seem to matter. I look into her eyes and find that there's something there that's farther away than the stars and brighter than the sun. Something that sings and cries and dreams and mourns. Something that's so close it suffocates and so remote that I'll never touch it.

"She's a witch. No broomstick. Only nightmares about a twin sister and compulsions to find a rainbow that leads to shimmering little heaps of fool's gold.

"She ran away. Three days ago she ran away, having

stolen one shot-gun, ten cartridges, half a dozen cans of soup and two of Miss Worrall's Alsatians. I wondered why she had been ingratiating herself so much with the dogs. She had been quietly planning the whole little venture.

"We went to bed around midnight and made some love that was quite worth the making, and then we slept. By dawn the bitch had gone. She'd taken the boat, of course, so I had to swim ashore. Then I had to row myself back to get a few things.

"I don't suppose I'd have found her except that I knew she'd head north. And, serve her right, the dogs gave her away. She should have realised that their occasional barking was going to be a first-class advertisement. But, thank the Lord, she didn't. And so I came up with them a little before sunset.

"She was wild enough and determined enough. She set the dogs on me, and I had to blow them both to glory—good dogs they were, too—before she'd call it a day.

"I hit her. Christ, how I hit her! I'd had about twelve hours of hell, thinking I'd never see her again. So she had to pay for it. I closed one of her eyes and smashed up her lips and did things to her that must have made her wish she'd never been born. And then I cried like a child and asked her to shoot me.

"How transnormal can you get? She didn't, of course. She could hardly move, but she just took her trousers off, maybe thinking that was the remedy for everything, or maybe thinking that was all I really wanted.

"I didn't want it at all. I told her I loved her, and then she began to cry, too. It was a fine night with a large harvest moon—if anybody was bothering to gather a harvest—and we slept rough at the bottom of a big tree with a couple of dead dogs to keep us company. We didn't make love at all. We just wanted to touch each other and know that we were alive.

"In the morning we were both stiff as boards, and poor Liz looked as if she had had the beating of a lifetime. She could hardly walk, and the way back was endless. We didn't get home till the early hours of the following morning. Then, if you please, instead of collapsing she had to have music.

"So it was *Rhapsody in Blue*, then bacon and red wine for breakfast. Finally, we went to bed.

"So here we are again, demented desert islanders, sharing a love idyll complete with black eyes, nightmares, blisters on our feet, aching loins and the knowledge that every day of joint survival, every moment of happiness (and who in his wrong mind would dare to use the word?) is stacking up the odds on the cosmic roulette wheel.

"It can't last. We know it can't last. Who can afford such delusions of grandeur in the world in which we live now? I know it's a sort of psychic hire-purchase—but, hell, we're going to have to pay later, anyway."

## SIXTEEN

DAY drifted into day, August drifted into September, and the brown and gold mantle of an Indian summer fell smokily over the land. Greville was surprised and only vaguely disturbed to find that life with Liz was evolving into a routine—or, possibly, a ritual. They went scrounging only when it was vitally necessary, when one of them needed clothes or shoes, or when the food supply began to dwindle seriously. For the most part they lived simply as "desert islanders". Liz still had her nightmares, still cherished hopes of finding Jane; but she seemed willing to accept Greville's claim upon her, and she seemed willing enough to share the dangerous illusion of love.

Inevitably, scrounging was getting more and more difficult, more and more dangerous. The towns and cities were still the best bets; but because sheer necessity was forcing the surviving transies to organise themselves into groups of one kind or another, the chance of free-lance scroungers falling into traps was increasing rapidly.

On one occasion Greville took Liz as far afield as Ipswich. They were looking primarily for clothes. In normal times the journey by car from Ambergreave would have taken about an hour; but because of the state of the roads and the detours it was necessary to make, the trip took the best part of a day.

The centre of Ipswich had been picked as clean as a whistle; but the suburbs still held the promise of plunder, for, having looted the centre of the city the town transies began to move progressively outwards. It was while Liz and Greville were exploring the possibilities of a large deserted suburban house standing in about two acres of garden jungle that they first encountered organised transnormality.

Greville had managed to force his station wagon up the weed-choked drive and it was standing in front of the house while he and Liz explored the upper storeys. The house was a solid nineteenth-century three-decker, complete with attic and trap door leading to a tiny fenced-in roof area. While Liz was trying on some rather old-fashioned clothes (chiefly evening-gowns and cocktail dresses) that she had found, Greville amused himself by going out on to the roof.

It was fortunate he did so, for he was able to observe the approach of about fifteen men. They did not approach haphazardly or with stealth as he would have expected ordinary transies to do. They marched three abreast behind a leader. Some of them carried shotguns, one or two had rifles and there were even a couple of spear men. The leader carried a sword and a pistol and looked for all the world like something that belonged more properly to the pages of *All Quiet On The Western Front*.

The entire troop was obviously well drilled for they marched briskly in step along the tracks left by Greville's car. Clearly they were proposing to investigate the intruders in their bailiwick.

Greville might have considered trying to talk himself out of trouble but he was not prepared to take risks with Liz. If there was a shortage of women in the area —and even if there wasn't—her prospects with a bunch of transnormal pseudo-soldiery would not be particularly rosy.

Fortunately Greville was well-armed. It was suicide to go on a scrounging expedition without being well-armed. So he was carrying rifle, pistol and grenades. Liz, still no doubt trying dresses on in front of a cracked mirror in one of the bedrooms, had a pistol and a shot-gun.

Greville gazed down at the approaching men below with an odd air of Olympian detachment. No doubt they had women and, perhaps, children dependent upon them. But in the transnormal world of the 1980s it was simply a question of *sauve qui peut.*

He flattened himself against a chimney-stack so that he would be hard to see, and took the pin out of one of his precious grenades. There was no time to warn Liz; and in any case, she would be aware of the situation quite soon enough.

He waited until the little group was about thirty yards from the car. Then he tossed the first grenade. He did not wait to see its effect but immediately withdrew the pin from a second grenade and dropped that, too. Luck —or whatever powers there were—was on his side. The first grenade dropped a little behind the men: the second grenade dropped a little ahead. There was hardly more than a second between the two explosions. Eight or nine of the men appeared to be killed instantly, a couple lay screaming and writhing and three who were only lightly wounded or mildly concussed picked themselves up and fled.

Greville thought their leader had been killed; but evidently he hadn't. He lay on the grass fumbling with his sword. Presently he raised it, displaying an off-white handkerchief knotted hastily on the end. Then he stood up. At the same time, Greville stood away from the chimney stack and called out to him. However, even as he shouted there was a flat, muffled crack. The man with the sword spun round and fell down. Liz had shot him from a bedroom window.

Greville went down to her. She was half in and half out of a green velvet cocktail dress.

"Come on," said Greville. "Grab your things. Our friends may have more friends. We'd better get out as fast as we can."

Liz grabbed a few of the dresses that lay at her feet and followed him downstairs, still trying vainly to zip up the green dress.

Outside, in the late sunlight, Greville briefly inspected the dead and dying. He gave the *coup de grace* quickly to two of the wounded, and hustled Liz into the car. Then he reversed the station wagon, drove at a recklessly high speed to the open road and headed back to Ambergreave.

They did not get home until very late, but Liz insisted on trying on all her new dresses for his approval before they went to bed. Greville was tired and nervous and depressed with his reaction to the afternoon's encounter. Luck would not be with them always. Sooner or later they, too, would be on the receiving end. He found to his surprise that he could contemplate his own death but he could not bear to think of Liz being killed.

"I hope you are satisfied with the dresses," he said brutally. "I hope they fit. And I hope you like the bloody colours. Dresses are getting quite expensive these days. That little lot cost a dozen men. Do you think they were worth the price?"

"Nothing is ever worth the price," retorted Liz calmly, "but it always has to be paid . . . Let's go to bed. After all, there's a price on that, too, isn't there?"

Greville didn't answer. He wanted to take her in his arms; but he was chilled by the knowledge that every day gave him more to lose.

## SEVENTEEN

It was the night of the first really heavy autumn fog, as Greville later recorded in his diary. It was a night for sitting by a log fire, reading, talking, listening to music, mending clothes, making impossible plans and finally dissolving the said plans in a deep and luxuriously warm sea of sleep. During the course of the night Liz and Greville managed to do all these things with a quiet satisfaction that might almost have amounted to happiness. And during the same night what was left of the village of Ambergreave began to die—violently and in a fashion bizarre even for the world of transnormality.

Greville had three clocks and no means of knowing the time. The second clock was always an hour ahead of the first clock, and the third clock was always an hour ahead of the second clock. When one stopped it could be reset by the others, when one gained or lost it could also be reset by the others. Thus, he argued, it was possible to maintain an arbitrary standard—and it was also possible to adjust the concept of time to one's personal convenience. If he got up late, he could look at the first clock and cherish the illusion that he had risen early. If he felt like going to bed early, he could look at the third clock and demonstrate that it was late. Actually he had long ago lost interest in clock time; though he still liked to feel it was available if he needed it. That was why he took care to wind the clocks regularly. It was a private joke that Liz could never understand.

Clock number three (Greville was in a going-to-bed early mood) struck midnight just as the shooting started. Greville stared at Liz; Liz stared at Greville. They were not particularly worried—merely interested, for the shooting sounded quite far away. And anyway they were separated from it by more than a hundred yards of water. Anyone who wanted to attack them would first of all have to find himself a boat.

"What the hell?" said Liz unconcernedly, as she endeavoured to thread a needle in order to sew a button on her shirt.

"Dogs," said Greville. "Just possibly rats, but dogs most likely. The fog has probably drawn them into the village. They'll be looking for easy pickings. They don't need vision as much as human beings do."

Liz shuddered, remembering her own encounter with dogs on Chelsea Bridge. "I hope they are in for a nasty surprise. To be eaten by dogs is bad enough, but to be eaten by dogs in a pea-soup—that's the absolute end."

Greville laughed. "The female mind never ceases to surprise me. If you're going to die, what does it matter whether you die in summer or winter, in sunlight or in fog?"

"A hell of a lot," retorted Liz. "When I die I want to be able to have a last look at something worth seeing . . . We'll have to go scrounging again pretty soon. I've got three working shirts and they're all dropping to pieces."

"I'm not going to risk a bullet in the belly just for shirts," said Greville. "We'll wait until there's a longer shopping list. Now stop making like the extinct suburban housewife and come to bed. We'll go and find out who has been eaten by the dogs tomorrow morning."

"Let's have some more music first," suggested Liz. Her appetite for music was beginning to be insatiable. They had already listened to Tchaikovsky's 1812 and the Rachmaninov Second Piano Concerto.

"Balls to music. We've had a surfeit. I want sex."

She smiled. "I'm hungry. It's a long time since we ate."

"Well, go and cut yourself a slice of ham while you're taking your knickers off. I'm tired."

"If you're tired, you won't want it."

"I'm not that tired."

There were more shots. They sounded farther away.

"Definitely dogs," said Greville. "If they meet the dogs at the windmill it should be quite an interesting duel. The badies won't know the goodies, but the goodies will have very strong ideas about the badies ... I wonder if Miss Worrall has forgiven you for stealing two of her Alsatians yet?"

"It was you who killed them," Liz pointed out.

"And it was you who tried to get them to kill me, you little bitch."

Greville stretched and yawned. The shooting seemed to have died away. "Now. You either come to bed or I drag you there. Which is it to be?"

Liz giggled. "A bit of both," she said.

But by the time Liz had eaten her fill of ham, the mood for making love had deserted him. It had given way to a disquieting tenderness. He simply wanted to hold Liz in his arms and abolish the world. In the end that was effectively what he did—for a few hours.

The fog was still there in the morning. There was nothing to do and nowhere to go, so they stayed in bed until hunger made them rise. Then they had a lazy breakfast and went back to bed again. This time they made love, for it was as if the fog had effectively and permanently cut them off from all humankind. It was as if they were entirely alone on the planet—so much alone that it was possible to entertain visions of unending isolation, of immortality and a closeness and interdependence so satisfying that it was almost painful.

There had been no more sounds of shooting to disturb their night. There were none to disturb the drugged sensual limbo of their morning. But by mid-afternoon the fog had cleared. Liz was prepared to declare the entire day a sexual holiday, but Greville was beginning to feel restless.

When the sun broke through, he had a sudden desire to get up and find out what had been happening in the outside world. He had a desire to see other people, to look at a world broader than that bounded by four bedroom walls.

Presently, he and Liz rowed away from their enchanted island. Now that the fog had cleared, the day was perfect in its autumn glory. There was not a breath of wind, and the leaves of all the trees round Ambergreave Lake—brown and bronze, orange and deep crimson—looked as if they might have been somehow riveted to the still air.

The landscape was motionless. In the low golden sunlight it seemed petrified—a fantastic and lovely vista of still life.

In the village of Ambergreave there were aspects of still-life also; but they contained nothing beautiful—only the hanging terror of violence, the obscene degradation of pain, the musty flavour of wanton destruction.

The first bizarre object Liz and Greville encountered was a body, a male, clothed in what was apparently a monk's habit. It lay untidily in the middle of the village street. The man's throat had been torn out. There was also a bullet wound in his chest.

Liz and Greville stared at each other. Instinctively they stepped back from the body and gazed warily at the nearby cottages. They saw nothing but the vacant eyes of windows. There was not a sound to trouble the still air.

Greville fingered his shot-gun nervously. He was surprised to find that his hands were wet with sweat. Death itself was not strange to him, nor was violence. But this was something absurd, something utterly grotesque.

"My God!" whispered Liz. "What a horrible mess!"

"Shut up and listen," snapped Greville. "And keep your gun handy."

But there was nothing to listen to—only a dreadful stillness, the frightening nullity of silence. They waited, motionless, expecting attack, expecting noise, expecting anything. There was nothing.

"All right," said Greville at length. "It won't come to us, so let's go and look for it. Keep about five paces behind me and watch the left-hand side of the street. I'll take the right. Something pretty bloody crazy has been going on."

They advanced cautiously along the street. Cottage after cottage spewed forth nothing but silence. It was as if, thought Greville, the whole village was transformed into a vacant film set.

Then they saw a head stuck on the end of a pole which had been fastened to a cottage gate. The head was Big Willie's head, grinning in death as it had often grinned in life. A message had been painted crudely in white on the roadway. Greville had the briefly hysterical illusion that Big Willie was trying to read it.

There were only four words: *Despair! The Lord commandeth.*

Greville muttered an obscenity and turned to Liz. She stared back at him, white-faced.

"Let's take a look inside the house," said Greville grimly, "and see if Big Willie's mother has also repented."

They went up to the cottage door. Greville kicked it open and rushed inside, shot-gun ready. He need not have worried.

Whether Big Willie's mother had repented of incest and probable cannibalism was now a point only of academic interest. She lay on the floor, her knees drawn up, her skirt thrown back, her ankles tied to her wrists, and with a wooden stake driven through her chest. She had not been a very old woman—probably, thought Greville, only in her late forties—and she had been quite handsome in a gipsy sort of way; with big dark eyes and prominent cheek bones.

Like Big Willie, her eyes were still open. But they did not register either amusement or pain. Only a horrible comic expression of infinite surprise.

There were two dead "monks" in the room. One had a knife in his back, the other had what presumably was a hatchet wound in his head, since a bloodstained hatchet lay nearby.

Liz had followed Greville into the cottage. He pushed her out again almost immediately. The scene, he felt, was not one to linger over.

"The hell with all this," he said roughly. "Let's see what has happened at the windmill."

Neither Big Willie nor his mother was an insupportable loss to the community. But Miss Worrall came under the heading of key personnel. Without her services as a grinder of corn it would be virtually impossible to make bread. Besides, Greville rather liked her. She seemed to him the kind of transie who was almost eccentrically normal.

The mill was on the far side of the village. Liz and Greville had to go down the entire length of the main street to get to it. They passed more corpses, including that of Charles Cuthbert the blacksmith, and three more pseudo-monks. Cuthbert had evidently had his throat cut. The "monks" appeared to have died variously of gun-shot wounds and dogs.

But the windmill itself was the scene of greatest devastation. It also presented the remains of what must have been quite a battle. Miss Worrall's Alsatians—Greville counted five of their bodies—had done phenomenal service, for they appeared to have accounted for at least twice their number of "monks".

The Alsatians had died of gun-shot wounds, knife wounds and sheer bludgeoning. The "monks" had died mostly of throat and facial wounds. In death, dogs and men seemed to be mingling almost affectionately—as if each was now regretting the excesses to which they had been driven by fear, blood-lust, pain and plain savagery.

The tower of the mill was of solid stone which Miss Worrall had covered with pitch a long time ago. The "monks"—at least, the survivors—evidently found such a permanent surface irresistible: they had painted more choice slogans upon it.

*Only God washes whiter than white* ... *Heaven has fewer vacancies* ... and, with final simplicity *Transies go home* ...

Neither Greville nor Liz paid much attention to the slogans, however. Their eyes were drawn to the windmill sails, now slowly and creakingly rotating in a barely perceptible breeze.

The sails had been used as a makeshift cross. Where they joined the hub and the hub joined the main spindle in the windmill cap, Miss Worrall hung. She had been crucified in the traditional manner.

Liz tried to be sick—but nothing would come. Greville wanted to find something—anything—and smash it to pieces.

It was fortunate he had his shot-gun ready, for as they gazed at the appalling sight he heard a low growl. A surviving Alsatian, dripping blood, seemed to drag itself in slow motion from inside the windmill. It summoned up its strength for a last onslaught—doubtless so crazed by pain it no longer knew or cared who was friend and who was enemy. It was as well that the Alsatian's reactions had been slowed down, for so had Greville's. He only just managed to shoot it in mid-air. The close range blast from the twelve-bore almost tore the dog in two. It was dead before it touched the ground.

Liz stopped trying to be sick and began to cry.

"Shut up!" said Greville. "Save it till later. This isn't the bloody time for luxuries."

Liz looked at him and shut up. As she did so, both of them became aware of another sound. It was like a long low animal moan that subsided in a fit of coughing. It seemed to come from inside the windmill. There was silence for a moment or two. Then it came again. This time it sounded human.

"There's one of the bastards left," cried Greville exultantly. "Maybe we can trade an eye for an eye."

Throwing caution aside, he ran to the open windmill door and scrambled up the wooden steps. Fearfully, Liz followed him.

There was nothing on the ground floor—nothing but a couple of sacks of corn, half a sack of flour and Miss Worrall's old piano. Greville ran upstairs to the second storey—Miss Worrall's bedroom and the sleeping quarters of her two favourite dogs. There was nothing there either.

The third storey was the grinding room. It contained the millstones, a pile of empty sacks—and the source of the noise that Liz and Greville had heard. One of the "monks" lay on the pile of sacks. There was blood on his face and—symbolically enough—blood on his hands.

Greville felt a sudden surge of satisfaction. Here, at least, was something that could be made to suffer for all that other suffering.

He raised his shot-gun. The man on the pile of sacks smiled faintly.

"Vengeance may prove somewhat inadequate," he said apologetically. "I rather think I'm already dying."

Greville was surprised as much by the voice as by its owner. He was no less surprised by the words.

"Maybe we can persuade you to put off that happy event for a little longer," snapped Greville. "Now who the hell are you and what were all the fun and games in aid of? And talk quickly and sensibly or I shall have the pleasure of blowing your hands and feet off one by one."

The man on the sacks did not appear to be greatly perturbed by the threat.

"I'd like some water," he said. "I'd never have believed I could feel so damned dry."

Greville turned to Liz who was standing behind him. "Get him some water. There's a pump just outside."

She went back down the stairs and returned a few moments later with an earthenware jug. The man on the sacks licked his lips.

Greville took the jug and went close to him. "Now, let's talk."

"The water first, please."

Greville poured some of the water on the floor at his feet.

"I said: Let's talk."

The wounded man half-stifled a moan. "Much good may it do you," he said weakly. "But as a point of what once might literally have been academic interest, you are being uncharitable to one Professor Francis Watkins, sometime holder of the chair of psychology at the late and not entirely lamented University of East Anglia ... Oh God! For Christ's sake kill me." The last words rose into a scream, and the scream brought a fresh trickle of blood from his lips.

Sadistically, Greville poured more water at the feet of Professor Francis Watkins. "Now tell us all about your religious persuasion," he said pleasantly. "If it sounds interesting, we might even give you a drink of water. If you can convince us that it's rather jolly to chop people up and crucify them, we might even be kind enough to finish you off. But don't bore us. We don't like to be bored."

Despite his ghastly appearance, and despite the pain, the man on the sacks managed to smile. "Anything is a fair trade for water," he murmured. "Sir, you are addressing a conscript lay member of the quite extraordinary order of the Brothers of Iniquity. I was starving and they fed me. I was useful and they let me live . . . The great joke is that I once had the effrontery to consider myself an authority on abnormal psychology." He began to laugh, but the laughter died into a thin, bubbly scream.

Suddenly Liz took the jug out of Greville's hand. She bent down, and cradled Professor Francis Watkins in her arms like an overgrown child. Then she gave him some water.

"Thank you, my dear. It hurts, you know. It hurts even to discover that there is compassion left in England today."

## EIGHTEEN

DESPITE his optimism—and in the circumstances it must have been justifiably described as such—Professor Francis Watkins, authority on abnormal psychology and temporary Brother of Iniquity, was not mortally wounded. A bullet had passed through his shoulder, another had ploughed through the top of his leg, and his arms and hands had been bitten by dogs. But with reasonable care, he would live.

That much Liz discovered when, regardless of Greville's obvious disgust, she ripped away the "monk's" habit and began to clean up the wounds as well as she could. The blood coming from Professor Francis Watkins's mouth was simply due to the fact that he had bitten his tongue rather badly when the wounds were still fresh and giving him quite a lot of pain.

Greville resented the man on the pile of sacks. He resented him because his own blood-lust was dying, because, caught between pity and hatred and revulsion, he was no longer sure of himself. Professor Francis Watkins was not a young man. He was fat and sixtyish and pathetic. He was the kind of transie to whom things were destined to happen simply because he completely lacked the art of avoiding anything. As some people are accident prone, this man was disaster prone. That, thought Greville, you could tell at a glance. If anything terrible was going to occur, he was the kind of man who would be naturally drawn to it as to a magnet.

The water revived him a little, and so did Liz with her inexpert ministrations. While she cleaned him up the tears streamed down his face in gratitude; and when he had got over the crying he began to pour out his story—regardless of the pain it caused his tongue—in a spontaneous act of confession.

While civilisation was collapsing upon itself, Professor Francis Watkins, whose own psychology turned out to be more abnormal than he had formerly supposed, retired to his library with stocks of food as large as he could muster, prepared to sit out what he had first regarded as only a temporary and rather interesting return to the Dark Ages.

But the Dark Ages got darker instead of lighter, the food store dwindled slowly away; and in the end he was forced to go out and risk his life—and, more important, the future of his library—for such delicacies as potatoes, turnips and, in the end, even carrion. He was no cook, but he had discovered that you could eat practically anything if you boiled it long enough.

The trouble was he was not much good at finding food. Sooner or later he would have to quit his beloved library or die in it of starvation. He could not drive a car, he could not fight and he could only just manage to pull the trigger of a gun. The wonder was that he had managed to survive it all.

Finally, when he had gone two days without food, an idea came to him. Civilisation had collapsed, but surely small centres of culture and learning must be flourishing somewhere? He just could not imagine a world in which all that he regarded of value had disappeared.

Granting, then, the existence of intelligent groups of people more fortunate than himself—people, doubtless whose primary concern would be the preservation of all that was worthwhile (to him, this only meant books) until the return of sane social organisation—it merely remained for him to find one of these groups, attach himself to it and wait patiently until the world was ready to appreciate the significance of Freud and Jung, of Adler and Pavlov, of Levtushenko and Eysenck once more.

That was the theory. It seemed a good theory. There was only one problem. Professor Francis Watkins had acquired one of the best private libraries on psychology in the whole of England. He did not want to abandon it. Indeed, it was his duty not to abandon it. Therefore he could either remain with it and die or take the best books with him. Unfortunately he had no means of transport.

But he was nothing if not a resourceful man. Hunger had sharpened his wits. He could not drive a car, but he could certainly push a small cart. If he could find a cart.

He couldn't. However, he found a substitute—or to be strictly accurate, he found three substitutes. They were perambulators that he discovered in a derelict baby-wear shop. They were the only forms of transport that he could lay his hands on.

So he filled them full of books. The choice was heartbreaking. Even loaded to overflowing, the perambulators could only carry about twenty per cent of the books that he considered essential for the foundation of a decent library in psychology.

And having filled the perambulators with his best books—the task of selection alone took him the best part of three days—he set off into the bright blue yonder. He didn't know where to go, but he felt that if he journeyed long enough in almost any direction sooner or later he would find sanctuary.

His method of progress was simple. He would push the first perambulator about a hundred yards, then he would come back for the second, and then for the third. Assuming that he could get enough food to keep body and soul together, he calculated that he would be able to cover five miles a day. At that rate, he told himself, it ought not to take longer than a month before he came across people who were similarly dedicated to keeping the intellectual achievements of the world alive.

There were only two flaws in the grand design. He didn't really know where he was going; and even if he did, he certainly couldn't find enough food to sustain him while he was getting there.

On the strength provided by about six pounds of very old potatoes and the rancid remains of a two-pound tin of butter, he wandered about for eight or nine days, meticulously pushing the first perambulator, going back for the second and then for the third. It was a miracle that he avoided being eaten by dogs or rats. And perhaps in doing so he had used up his entire ration of miracles.

For, having consumed the last of his potatoes and the last of his butter, he suddenly realised that he was not going anywhere at all, and lay down to die. It was then that the Brothers of Iniquity found him.

If he had been more than half alive, they would have killed him. As he was obviously more than half dead, they did their best to save him. Their best consisted simply of giving him food and keeping him warm. For a day or two he raved, believing that, surrounded as he was by tonsured heads and robes of Hessian and even sack-cloth, he had truly arrived back in the Dark Ages. But then he grew lucid and began to get better.

So the Brothers of Iniquity shaved his head, provided him with a monk's habit and initiated him as a compulsory novice. The initiation rites of the Brothers of Iniquity were simple and exceedingly effective; the novice was forced to do what he most disliked doing. Men who were physical cowards were forced to fight against veterans of the Order with knives, razors or bottles. Men who were naturally courageous were made to endure all kinds of indignities without the means of retaliation. Men who were normally sexed were handed over to a group of homosexuals. Men who could not swim were thrown into a river. Men who could not bear to be alone were given a period of solitary confinement. And so on. Every man had his Achilles' heel, and every man was subject to public exposure and degradation.

Professor Francis Watkins was not greatly interested in women, so the Brothers of Iniquity produced for him a half-starved nymphomaniac whom they had acquired in their travels and neglected to rape or kill only because she would have welcomed both or either.

The nymphomaniac, a gaunt and physically strong woman who looked about twice her actual age, was given a bottle of whisky and the promise of solid food for every successful completion of the sexual act that she could achieve with Professor Francis Watkins. The two of them were locked in a cellar for a day and a night—at the end of which time Professor Francis Watkins was hysterical and the woman had earned a credit of three meals. The degradation was witnessed by a senior Brother, who kept a long but somewhat entertaining vigil for the purpose.

This, however, was only the first part of the initiation. The Brothers had noted that, above all, Professor Francis Watkins wished to preserve his books. So they made him burn them. It was the only occasion on which he attempted to display courage. He refused to light the bonfire and told them that they could kill him first.

The Brothers of Iniquity had no intention of killing him. They merely offered him the choice of burning the books or spending an unspecified time locked up with the nymphomaniac. He decided to burn his books. Anything seemed preferable to the kind of rape that had not, to the best of his knowledge, been documented or even suggested in the books he was about to destroy.

It was only afterwards, when his spirit was broken, that he realised there were compensations in belonging to the Brothers of Iniquity. The Order, though not unique in history, was certainly unique in modern times. It embodied a form of mania that was in itself fascinating. For the Brothers of Iniquity were dedicated to the propositions that God was mad, cruel and utterly absurd.

God, they believed (or, at least, the fanatics among them believed), had brought about Omega radiation and the radiant suicide simply because man was in danger of developing a rational, healthy and flourishing society. Further, they believed that God had purposely left the process of destruction incomplete because he wished to offer redemption to the chosen. The chosen were, of course, the Brothers of Iniquity. It was their mission to complete God's work among the lesser mortals; and when they had completed the task of cleansing the planet they would then be able to enjoy the ultimate privilege of destroying themselves. At which point, according to their theologians, they were destined for immortal madness in some indescribably psychotic heaven until God should choose to have more interesting nightmares and clothe them with substance in some far and infinitely absurd anti-Eden.

The surprising thing was not that transnormals should develop such ideas but that so many transnormals should be capable of organising themselves so effectively; for the Brothers of Iniquity were numbered now in hundreds. Their mortality rate was high; but so was their rate of recruitment. And their leader, who called himself Brother Lucifer, had the kind of demagogic quality that earlier tyrants might have envied.

Adopting the proposition that life, being God-given, was absurd, he sought to magnify its absurdity by pursuing absolute frustration along a path of random acts. He permitted the Order to indulge in ritual cannibalism because of its absurdity; but death by torture was the fate of anyone who dared to eat pork because he decreed that pigs, being almost perfectly absurd, were therefore sublime and possibly the purest manifestation of God's will. On one occasion he had even sacrificed about a hundred of the brethren in a forlorn attempt to save half a dozen pigs from a very large pack of dogs.

After a time, and humiliated though he was by the constant indignities heaped upon him in accordance with the precept of absolute frustration, Professor Watkins began almost to enjoy his experiences in a masochistic sort of way. He was in a unique position for field-work, he felt. He had still not abandoned hope that sooner or later the nightmare would end and that somehow he would once again find his way into a world of academic peace and security; but meanwhile he, the trained observer, would record the basic, naked manifestations of human madness and depravity. Some day he would be able to write about it. Some day he would be able to evaluate what had happened and perhaps use his knowledge to do what no one else had ever been able to do before—to evaluate, by negative reference, the basic criteria of sanity.

But then he was overtaken by the random consequences of Iniquitism. The Brothers, lost in a fog, discovered Ambergreave and decided to sanctify it by their attentions. It was the first time Professor Francis Watkins had seen the philosophy of the Brothers of Iniquity put into practice on a large scale. He was terrified by what he saw. He was also badly bitten; and, in a state of moral and physical collapse, had hidden himself in the windmill, hoping that the Brothers would go away and leave him. But one of them found him before the company departed. When he would not move, and because he seemed to be wounded, he was shot twice for good measure and left to die in his own time.

This was the story he told Greville and Liz, while taking grateful sips of water and easing himself into a comfortable position. Greville had thought that nothing could surprise him any more. He was wrong. Professor Francis Watkins could and did surprise him. Give or take a little, thought Greville, there but for the grace of sheer chance go most of us.

"I would add," said Professor Francis Watkins, smiling wanly, "that despite the care of your good lady, my own stupid constitution and your commendable patience, I would be much obliged if you would discharge that instrument of destruction in such a way as to provide me with the minimum of pain and a fairly rapid demise ... I—I rather fear I have seen a little too much."

"Where are the Brothers of Iniquity now?" asked Greville.

The old man shrugged. "Who knows. They went to

the south—that is, I believe, towards Thetford—but sheer whim could take them anywhere." He shuddered. "It could even bring them back here ... Now, if you would be so kind as to aim carefully and press the trigger ... I really think I would be much obliged, you know."

If he had pleaded for life, Greville would probably have shot him. But he was pleading for death and, perhaps affected by a philosophy of absurdity himself, Greville refused to grant the final luxury.

He gave Liz an inquiring look. She nodded.

"We're taking you home," said Greville. He laughed grimly. "After all we have our own standards of iniquity to consider."

Professor Francis Watkins started crying again.

## NINETEEN

Francis—for so they came to call him—took quite a long time to recover from his wounds. Being an oldish man, unused to exertion or privation, he did not have much stamina. Nor did he have any will to live. Because of this, and out of sheer perversity, Greville determined that he should live. What was to be done with an ex-professor of psychology, Greville did not know; nor did he care to look very much into the future, for he had a presentiment that, somehow, time was running out.

The trouble was that he, who had managed alone and had been aloof for so long, had allowed himself to become emotionally involved with mankind once more in the person of Liz. He loved her as he had never loved Pauline. He loved her enough to be more afraid for her than for himself. They had got over the stage of wanting to take from each other and had learned to give to each other. It was a delicious, agonising, heady sort of feeling. It was a mad honeymoon in a nightmare world. Above all, it was a relationship that was utterly vulnerable ... And now there was Francis ... And suddenly the cottage on the island that was big enough for two was overcrowded. The citadel had become an open city. The hard world of reality, disguised as an old man with bullet wounds and dog bites, had entered by insane invitation through the back door.

They had carried Francis from the windmill to the edge of the lake in a wheelbarrow. They had ferried him across to the island, taken him into the cottage and dumped him on the bed that had so recently been a bed of love. That, thought Greville, as he levered the old man on to sheets that still bore the imprint and even the warmth of recent love and tenderness, was symbolically the end of the honeymoon. There would, with luck, be other times; but they would never again be like the times that had gone.

It was still daylight though the sun was already sinking through a quiet sky. Greville told Liz that he was going to go back to Ambergreave and explore a bit more systematically.

"But what if those bloody maniacs come back?" protested Liz.

"That's one of the things I want to find out," said Greville. "My guess is that the fog saved us last night. If they'd known there was an island in the lake, an island with a house on it, very likely they'd have had a go. According to our friend, they have pushed off towards Thetford. He may be right, but it would be damn stupid not to check on it. I'll take the car and drive a little way along the Thetford road. I just want to make sure they aren't going to double back."

"You'll be careful?"

"Of course, I'll be careful. What the hell! Do you think I want to get myself hammered?" Greville's irritability served to disguise his anxiety.

"I don't know," retorted Liz. "Transies do stupid things, don't they?"

Greville held her to him for a moment, then went out of the cottage. Life, he thought, was a crazy affair. You could spend years teaching yourself not to care about any damn thing in the world. You could witness suicide, murder, mayhem, starvation, disease and massacre and remain reasonably detached. Then suddenly you were flung head first into a mud-bath of emotion. You struggled in it, you wallowed in it and finally you ended up drowning in it—and caring like hell about every god-damned inconsequential tragedy in an inconsequential world.

He rowed ashore, checked his guns and started the car. Then he drove slowly through Ambergreave, gazing at the horror and desolation that surrounded him in the now fading light, and feeling like a lone survivor in a world irrevocably committed to putrefaction and death.

It was some time since he had felt so lonely. The day was still quite warm, but it was some time since he had felt so cold. The sails of the windmill were still rotating slowly, and what was left of Miss Worrall was rotating with them. Suddenly he could not bear the sight. He stopped the car and got out.

After a few minutes of searching, he discovered Miss Worrall's carefully hoarded store of paraffin. She had about thirty gallons left. He poured three-quarters of it on the ground floor of the mill and took the rest outside to splash on the sails as they came round. Then he used one of his precious matches to light the funeral pyre. It blazed up quickly and the sails began to burn like some monstrous Catherine wheel, flinging off sparks and bits of timber. The stone shell of the windmill acted like a chimney and drew the fire inside until the roaring and the heat made Greville stand well back.

Setting fire to the mill was a fool thing to do, he decided. But he felt better for having done it. He waited until the sails came crashing down, bringing what was left of Miss Worrall to be incinerated in their midst, then he started the car once more and drove cautiously along the Thetford road.

He drove about five miles and discovered only two wounded Brothers of Iniquity resting by the roadside. Doubtless they were hoping to overtake the main body by nightfall.

Neither of them had weapons and, in fact, it would probably not have made a great deal of difference if they had. They were both weakened by pain and loss of blood. They were lying on a thick patch of grass round a bend, and Greville was already driving past before he noticed them. He stopped the car about fifty yards further on, and hurled himself out on the theory that he might have walked into an ambush.

He waited, but nothing happened. Then he picked himself up and, shot-gun in hand, walked back towards the two men. They saw him coming. One of them tried to crawl away, but the other was too weak or too stiff to move.

Greville felt inclined to indulge himself in melodrama. He stopped about five yards from them. The man who was trying to crawl gave up the attempt and turned to face him.

"Stand up," said Greville.

They both tried, but neither of them could make it.

"The sentence of this court," said Greville, "is that you shall have a little time for reflection."

He shot each of them at close range in the stomach. Then, unmoved by the resulting screams, he turned the car round and drove slowly back in the direction of Ambergreave.

## TWENTY

EACH day for a few days after the massacre at Ambergreave Greville made probing sorties in different directions—chosen more or less at random. On two occasions he discovered small villages through which the Brothers had obviously and recently passed, leaving behind them a swathe of destruction similar to the one they had left at Ambergreave; but he did not encounter any more of them alive. They seemed to be heading generally south, perhaps making for London. Greville rather hoped that this was the case, because he felt that in London or its environs they stood a reasonable chance of encountering opposition that would prove too big for them to handle. The worst fate he could wish upon them was not that they should encounter a larger and better armed group of humans but simply that they should receive the attention of a horde of rats—preferably very hungry rats, and preferably at night.

Meanwhile, despite his age and lack of stamina, Francis continued to improve. Among his treasures in the cellar, Greville had a large store of exceedingly old and quite useless penicillin tablets. These he fed to Francis like sweets, and the old man developed a liking for them since they had the vestiges of a synthetic orange flavour. They didn't appear to do him any harm and just possibly may have done him a little good.

Greville allowed Francis to continue to occupy the bed in which he and Liz had created their private world of ecstasy. The bedroom became Francis's private territory. Greville had found a massive four-poster in one of the derelict houses of Ambergreave. Section by section he hauled it down to the lake and floated it across to the island. Further scrounging provided him with a foam rubber mattress.

The four-poster was magnificent, hand-carved and obviously very ancient. When it was assembled in the living room Liz was so delighted with it that she made a canopy and curtains for it. The bed completely dominated the room, and in the evenings when Francis had tactfully retired to his own territory, Liz and Greville, feeling mildly sinful, would build up a large fire and retire to bed content simply to talk and look at the flames. Then, after a time, Greville would draw the curtains and effectively reduce the cosmos to a cube enclosing one man and one woman.

But despite a sufficiency of food and the double luxury of sex that had generated love, the outside world could not wholly be ignored. The autumn was deepening, the days were growing shorter, Liz was getting more frequent nightmares about Jane, the odds against survival were steadily lengthening, and across a few yards of water the village of Ambergreave lay mute, stinking and desolate—a constant reminder that what had happened yesterday would probably be repeated with variations tomorrow. Mankind, or what was left of it, had turned cannibal just as much as the pigs and the rats. The surviving transies were living off the past and off each other. And because of this they were clearly doomed. Sooner or later their numbers would become critically low; and then, no doubt, man would join the dodo and the phoenix to become a legend in a world where there was no one to take any notice of legends.

Left to his own devices, Greville might have been content to live from day to day, taking each day as it came, merely thankful for another twenty-four hours of grace. But there was Francis. And if Greville had been tempted ever to regard his island as a kind of shabby Eden, Francis would most certainly have been cast for the role of serpent.

"You know," said Francis one afternoon when they were sitting out of doors, enjoying an hour of late sunlight, "what saddens me most is that there probably aren't enough people left to care."

"To care about what?" asked Greville. He was watching Liz pluck a chicken—one that had signed its own death warrant by refusing to lay—and he was marvelling that it was possible to turn such a mundane act as plucking a chicken into a sequence of movements that had grace, charm and an oddly symbolic kind of promise.

"About the future of man," said Francis sombrely. "It's easy to care about individual futures, easiest of all to care about our own. But it's damned difficult to care about an abstraction ... It's such a pity, really. We spent about half a million years growing self-consciousness, language and conceptual thought. Then we spent another half million years learning what to do with them. Then the sun gets an itch in its belly, the irritation gets radiated across a hundred million miles of space and triggers off the death-wish in three thousand million creatures, each of whom is potentially greater than the sun simply because the sun can neither laugh nor cry."

Greville, absorbed in Liz, who was absorbed in the chicken, had only been listening vaguely.

"There are still a few people left who can laugh and cry," he said.

Francis sighed. "Yes, but can any of them care? Can any of them really care? Do any of them want to care? I'm just a tired old man full of worn out paranoia and I would like to feel that somewhere somebody cared."

"Why?" asked Greville.

"So that an ape with a soul that gibbered for the moon and died with a tool in its hand will not have died in vain. I'm a romantic, I know, but this is an ignominious way for mankind to go out. Better to have had the sun turn into a nova, better to have died to a man of some insidious and unconquerable disease. Better even to have blown ourselves to glory for the sake of ideas . . . But not like this. It's so futile, so untidy."

"Yes," said Greville bitterly. "We had a great civilisation. We had nuclear weapons, bacteriological warfare and brain-washing. One-third of us developed heart diseases from overeating and two thirds of us developed other diseases from malnutrition. It was a hell of a civilisation! We had hot lines from Washington and London to Moscow and Peking. But there weren't any hot lines from the slums of Bombay to New York. You could have your nose reshaped or your double chin removed for a mere five hundred pounds at the London Clinic, but in Central Africa we let them die of beriberi, malaria, leprosy and plain hunger for free."

Francis smiled. "Dear lad, for a transie you are beginning to sound abnormally normal . . . Of course there was injustice. Of course there was tyranny and fear and tremendous waste. And what do you think the answer could have been? Communism, Utopianism, humanism or any other -ism? Well I can tell you that -isms never got anybody anywhere. The moment you have an -ism you begin to freeze ideas. Orthodoxy evolves into tyranny, and then you are back to—what was the phrase?—square one. No, Greville, my friend; what humanity needed was simply time. Another ten thousand years of it. Not much to ask, really, from a cosmic point of view. But the sun had indigestion, and here we are. I suppose it's funny, in a way, but my sense of humour isn't what it was."

Greville was enjoying the argument. He knew it was going nowhere, because there was nowhere for it to go. But he was enjoying it. He had not endeavoured to solve the problems of the world for nearly twenty years, and now that they were past solving he felt he could almost achieve an Olympian detachment. There were no problems to solve now—apart from the ordinary personal ones. All that remained was to render a verdict.

"Humanity," he said, "wasn't worth another ten thousand years. It was rotten."

Francis, too, was enjoying himself. It was a long time since he had held a tutorial. "So Beethoven was rotten?

And Buddha and Leonardo da Vinci, and Socrates, and —coming a bit nearer home—Dag Hammarskjold and Albert Schweitzer?"

Greville laughed. "Transies," he said, "crazy mixed-up transies. They suffered from delusions of grandeur —and so did Attila, Jenghiz Khan, Julius Caesar, Napoleon, Hitler, Stalin ... And even Jesus Christ ... Transies all ... Exceedingly dangerous specimens in a world of latter-day apes."

Francis permitted himself a display of indignation that he did not actually feel. "The trouble with you is that you are afraid to admit what has been lost. You are afraid of admitting anything because if you did it would move you to tears ... Yes, we butchered people in the twentieth century as we butchered them throughout history. We butchered their minds and bodies. But at the same time sight was being restored to the blind, hearing to the deaf, limbs to the disfigured or the malformed. We could make one voice heard across the planet, one orchestra could play to three continents. We could set down thinking machines on the face of the moon. What we lost when the sun decided to have celestial hiccoughs was not so much a few thousand million people as a vision of greatness ... We could have been great, you know. In time we could even have been great enough to enter the mind of God."

"Now I know why you survived," retorted Greville. "You're just another frustrated bloody saviour. You lived in a little academic world and did crosswords with the Almighty and didn't have erections because you thought they were just a shade uncouth. You're just an ape with a computer complex. You think that because you've got a few million grey cells sitting on top of your spine you're more special than a tree. How the hell do you know that a tree isn't more perfectly designed to enter what you grandly call the mind of God?"

"Because," said Francis, "a tree is never more than a tree. But there have been moments when men have been greater than man ... The perennial ape I grant you. Grant me in return a few concepts that could have justified the existence of life on this burnt-out cinder whirling stupidly round a dyspeptic star."

"Hot or cold?" inquired Liz. She had finished plucking the chicken, and it was her first contribution to the conversation.

"I beg your pardon?" said Francis.

"I said: hot or cold?"

"We are temporarily deserting the mind of God to consider the future of a dead chicken," explained Greville drily. "Liz is less intellectual than practical. You and I may discuss the now theoretical potential of mankind, but she will see that our bellies are filled while we are doing it. She is also good for sexual solace, and that, more than anything, keeps away the eternal cold."

Liz surveyed them both. "A woman gave birth to each of you," she said. "I expect it was a pretty energetic process. Let's hope the original screw was more satisfying than the end product ... Now, hot or cold?"

"Hot," said Francis.

"Cold," said Greville.

Liz grinned. "You're both a couple of liars." She picked up the chicken and took it into the house.

Greville watched her go, and felt his heart ache.

Francis watched Greville. "She's right, you know. We are a couple of liars. You don't believe what you say any more than I do." Then he could not resist adding a trifle maliciously, "On the other hand, it appears there are still a few things that have not been lost."

## TWENTY-ONE

EXTRACT from Greville's diary:

"October. Day ninety—a piece of precision I allow myself as a slight luxury. It's not accurate, of course. I never stick at any damn thing, even the memoirs of a semi-retired grave-digger.

"Francis is dead. He wasn't with us long enough to matter. And yet he mattered. What was it about him? He was just another sad, lonely creature, an absurd old man with a headful of abstractions and three-syllable words. He wasn't programmed for survival. He was even too stupid to look after himself properly. He would go for days without washing. If Liz hadn't forced a minimum routine of hygiene on him he would have worn all his clothes until they stank—or fell off in rags. He was lazy, he was impractical, he was pompous. And yet ... And yet I liked him. Why the hell should I feel so affectionate for somebody who was so absurd? My trouble is that I'm learning how to care. It's dangerous.

"Francis was absurd enough to die absurdly for an absurd reason. Or maybe there were two reasons. Because I shall never know whether he died for the Concise Oxford Dictionary or for a half-starved boy in cat skins. I suppose it was my fault, really. I shouldn't have indulged him. After all, what was he? Nothing more than a piece of human wreckage that Liz persuaded me to save against my better judgement.

"All right, Greville, my lad! Make like God! Offer your divine verdict on one more machine that failed!

"The truth is there is no verdict to be offered upon Francis, except the customary open verdict. I liked him, that's all.

"It happened on a scrounging expedition. Liz and I had the usual kind of shopping list—food, clothes, guns, ammunition, petrol, paraffin. But all Francis wanted was books. I told him there would probably be no time left to look for books, but he wanted to come anyway. He probably had a theory he could persuade me to make time. He succeeded—and died.

"We'd had quite a bit of luck, really, The car was running well, the roads we chose (or what was left of them) didn't have any nasty surprises, and the weather was fine. I determined to avoid towns and villages as much as possible. Isolated houses, preferably large ones—and preferably uninhabited—were the main targets. We didn't want to fight anybody. We just wanted loot. But if it came to fighting, we were as prepared as we could be: one rifle, one revolver and two shot-guns. We weren't too badly off for ammunition, since I'd found a little in what the Brothers of Iniquity had left of Ambergreave.

"The first couple of houses that we tried had been picked clean as a bone. The third one was inhabited, and we were lucky enough to be able to reverse the car and get the hell out of it before the shooting became accurate. But the fourth house was a gold mine. It was difficult to understand why someone had not cleaned it out before us. Maybe it was too secluded. We only discovered it by accident. Liz spotted what looked like a narrow track leading into a wood; and there at the end of it was the house.

"Our total haul was three pairs of trousers, five shirts, several blankets, a couple of evening gowns (circa 1960), a dozen or so unlabelled tins (later we found they all contained fruit juice), a couple of oil lamps, various woodworking tools and about six or seven gallons of paraffin at the bottom of a forty-gallon drum. Fortunately we had brought a couple of empty five-gallon cans with us.

"The next house we found was even better. It was nearby and had probably once been a gamekeeper's cottage. There we got a rusty shot-gun, a box of candles, a large jar of pickled onions, two small jars of jam, three boxes of matches (damp, but they were all right when we dried them out), an old sheepskin jacket and about a hundred pounds of flour. The flour had been stored in earthenware jars—God knows how long—but it was still fresh and dry. It was the jackpot.

"Francis helped us load all our spoils in the station wagon and said casually: 'How about going back by Bury St. Edmunds? It's the shorter route.'

" 'Too dangerous,' I said. 'I don't like towns, these days. We'll go back the way we came. Then we'll have no trouble.'

" 'There's a public library in Bury,' said Francis diffidently. There may still be a few interesting books left.'

" 'Fuck the books. You can't eat them.'

"Francis sighed. 'Metaphorically, one can, of course. That's what books are for.'

"Surprisingly, Liz supported Francis. But I overruled the pair of them. We set off back the way we came. We weren't so lucky on the way back. We hit a road block.

"Maybe the people who manned it had heard us go through the first time and guessed that we were on a scrounging expedition. Or maybe they just set up blocks at random intervals.

"The block in this case was nothing more than a very old tractor that more or less filled the narrow lane. Whoever set it up had chosen a bad place because although it was round a bend, I still had about twenty-five yards' warning. Enough to stop the car, reverse it round the bend and make a turn of sorts. We got away even before the shooting started.

"But, to the delight of Francis, the only alternative route back to Ambergreave that I knew led through Bury St. Edmunds. It was late afternoon. Soon it would be dusk. I thought the risk was worth taking.

"There was no trouble in the outskirts of Bury. It seemed like a ghost town. We drove on until we came to the market square. Still no trouble.

"And there was the public library, and here was Francis in the car, pining for a few miserable books.

"'Give me five minutes—only five minutes,' he pleaded. 'Man does not live by bread alone. Besides, the whole place is deserted. Who in their right minds would want to live here?'

"I was inclined to agree with him. 'Look,' I said. 'I'm going to park in the middle of the square so that if anybody wants to shoot they'll have to shoot from a distance. I'm not going to get out of the car and neither is Liz. We'll cover you as well as we can, but you'd better make it quick.'

"'Greville, my friend,' said Francis, nearly falling over himself in his eagerness to get out of the car, 'you are almost a civilised transnormal. One should not allow an educated mind to starve. It's the worst kind of vandalism.'

"'Three minutes,' I said. 'You talk too much.'

"Beaming all over his face, Francis ran across the square like a child of another age heading for the school tuck-shop.

"Liz and I sat side by side, each with a shot-gun ready to poke out of either window. There's a special art in shooting from a car. By then, even Liz was getting good at it. But there was nothing to shoot at. Night was coming down, the world was quiet and, for all we could tell, we were the only people in the vicinity.

"I was glad of the fading light. The car seemed horribly exposed, standing in the middle of the square. But that was the best place to be. Anyone who wanted to investigate would have to cover about forty yards of open ground: anyone who wanted to shoot from the cover of the nearest building could barely see his target.

"Liz shivered. 'We're not alone,' she said.

" 'How do you know?'

" 'I can feel it.'

" 'Does your extra-sensory perception extend to knowing where the opposition is?'

" 'No.'

" 'Then concentrate on it.'

"Francis had taken a small rechargeable electric torch with him. We could see the dancing glow it cast on the inside walls of the library. Many of the windows were broken. I had a feeling he would be a bit disappointed. Rats would have disposed of most of the books.

"It seemed a long time, but it was probably only two or three minutes, before he returned, staggering, with a pile of books. He dumped them in the back of the station wagon, piling them untidily on the rest of our treasures.

" 'There's not much left,' he said, puffing from his exertions. 'The *Britannica* seems to be reasonably untouched, though. Another couple of trips and I'll have the rest of the volumes.'

" 'What the devil do you want an encyclopaedia for?' I asked irritably.

" 'What the devil do you want to go on living for?' retorted Francis.

" 'You'd better be quick, then. Liz seems to think we are not alone.'

" 'Good,' said Francis equably. 'Loneliness is not conducive to happiness.' He trotted back to the library.

"The second trip did not take so long.

" 'I heard noises,' he said unconcernedly, as he dumped his load of books. He chuckled. 'Maybe it's a late borrower in the fiction department.'

" 'Get in We're pulling out.'

" 'Not until I have the rest of *Britannica*.' And off he went again.

"The minutes passed. He was a long time coming

back. I was just about to go and haul him out when I saw his unmistakable, book-laden bulk in the semi-darkness.

"He pushed the books among the rest of our loot. 'Guess what!' he said excitedly. 'I've found a boy dressed in skins.'

" 'That's nice,' I said. 'Now get in. We've been here far too long.'

" 'No,' said Francis. 'I've just remembered. I need a good dictionary . . . The boy's starving. Do you think—'

" 'No, I don't bloody well think. Now get in the car before I shoot you.'

"Francis laughed. 'Never make a threat you don't propose to carry out. Just one more minute. I know exactly where the dictionary is . . . About the boy. Perhaps we might just—'

" 'We might just nothing!' I snapped angrily and pointed the shot-gun at him. 'Now get in before I blow you to glory.'

"Francis sighed. 'Sorry to be a nuisance. I'll just get the dictionary.' And off he went.

"I felt like shooting him. I felt like beating his silly brains out with a gun butt. I did nothing but sit and wait and fume.

"Liz attempted to soothe me in an odd sort of way. 'What does it matter? What does anything matter? Don't get worked up about him, love. He's got to have something to take to bed at nights.' She giggled 'Even if it is only a dictionary."

"And suddenly I felt sorry for anyone and everyone who did not have his Liz.

"Presently Francis emerged from the library. He was carrying more than the dictionary. There was an indistinct but vaguely human shape in his arms. He staggered a little, and I would have got out to help him—except that I was feeling too damned angry again. Hell, I'd saved the man's life, and he didn't give a damn about what I thought or felt or wanted. I let him struggle across the square with his armful of skin and bones. I couldn't see the child very well, and I was thinking that pretty soon I might just as well turn my little cottage into a combined vagrancy hostel and orphanage.

"Francis had almost reached the car when somebody

—by luck or good management—did an excellent bit of shooting.

"At the same time, Liz thought she saw a movement on the far side of the square and banged away with her shot-gun. So did I. Both barrels. Somebody screamed.

"Then I turned to look at Francis. He had dropped to his knees, still clutching his sad little bundle of humanity. He looked as if he was staying upright by sheer will-power. I jumped out of the car and ran to him. Liz was still shooting.

"Francis had a boy of perhaps nine or ten in his arms. The dictionary had fallen to the ground.

" 'Sorry, dear lad,' said Francis. '*Deus ex machina.* Very fitting . . . The boy's all right?'

" 'The boy's fine,' I assured him, and took the little heap out of his arms.

" 'I've had it,' said Francis. 'Keep our Neanderthal friend as a souvenir . . . The poor child couldn't move . . . I found him with a home-made bow and two arrows, if you please.' He sank down on his haunches and grinned. 'He was trying to read *Grimm's Fairy Tales* by candlelight.'

" 'I'll get you back to the car,' I said.

" 'No good . . . Take the boy . . . And, Greville—'

" 'Yes?'

" 'Love somebody . . . Build something.' Francis made a low and terrible kind of growling noise. Then he flopped back in an untidy heap.

"I looked at the child I was holding. The bullet had passed right through Francis and struck him in the back of the head.

"He could have been about ten, I suppose. He was wearing a single garment made of cat skins, and he looked as if he'd been starving for months. Probably he wouldn't have lived long anyway.

"I looked at Francis, then I looked at the child once more. Oddly, the child's face seemed much older. It looked as if it had already endured all the miseries of man.

"Francis was dead and the child was dead, and Liz was banging away with her shot-gun as if it was the glorious twelfth.

"'The boy's fine,' I babbled, as I laid him down by the side of Francis. 'He'd like to stay with you a while, just to keep you company.'

"Then I came to my senses, and dashed back to the car. And I started the engine and got the hell out of it quick. Liz never saw what she was shooting at. Maybe they never saw what they were shooting at, either."

## TWENTY-TWO

THE frosts came, bringing with them the sharp and antiseptic flavour of winter. The landscape died in hoary splendour. Leaves drifted into bleak, undisturbed mountains, dead wood fell, and the November world hung grey with loneliness.

In an odd way the death of Francis sobered Greville and Liz. It frightened them more than the destruction of Ambergreave had done, more than any of the bizarre or pointless killings they had witnessed—or brought about—since they came together. It frightened them because Francis had come to belong to them, because, having accepted him in their intimate world, they had unconsciously bestowed upon him their own unconscious assumptions of immortality.

True, they lived in the shadow of violence and had some experience of the art of murder; true also that they were conscious—Greville particularly so—that each day of continued existence was a welcome and possibly unmerited bonus. But none of this really compelled them to accept the fact of their own mortality.

The death of Francis did. For, in the short time that they had known him, Francis had become a part of them; and a part of them had died.

It was impossible now to retire to their little cottage on the island and shut out the world. It was impossible because the world entered in the form of a ghost. Invisibly, Francis listened to their music. Silently, he took issue with Greville's more dogmatic statements. And there was even mute laughter when Liz uttered one of her habitual *non sequiturs*. Greville would not have believed it possible that one who was dead could be so insistently and negatively alive.

The gaiety was gone, the fantasy could no longer be maintained. Even in the act of love there was only desolation. Skeletons seemed to be rattling inside the passionate flesh: intimations of oblivion defied Beethoven, alcohol, food and orgasm.

Greville could not understand why an old man whom they had only known briefly should affect them so much. He could not understand why an invisible sentinel should bar all the familiar avenues of escape.

"Love somebody," Francis had exhorted, dying. "Build something."

Well, there was someone to love—though love itself was a most painful luxury. But what was there to build? What could you create in a world that was dying, that was surrendering all its illusions of greatness to the primal law?

You could build nothing but a pyramid of memories —the glory that was supermarkets, the grandeur that was launderettes. Physically and emptily potent, Greville became despondent with awareness of his spiritual impotence. And the despondence was infectious.

The nightmares that had plagued Liz returned with greater intensity. Jane was another ghost, inhabiting the colourful drowned world of darkness. Jane was Liz, and Liz was Jane; and together they endured the twilight terrors of being alone in a nocturnal madhouse where lust and cruelty were the only signs of human companionship.

One morning Liz could stand it no longer. She gave Greville his breakfast then pointed a loaded pistol at him.

"I'm going away," she said calmly. "You can come with me, but you can't stop me. If you think you'll humour me by coming and then bring me back at the first opportunity, you'll probably succeed. But then I shall just have to kill you and start out again . . . I tried once before. You stopped me, and I was glad you stopped me. But not this time." Her voice faltered a little. "I'm playing it for real."

Greville looked at the pistol, then proceeded to finish his meal without hurrying. Liz had become a passing fair cook. The "bacon" tasted like vintage bacon, the free-range egg was far more acceptable than any egg he had ever bought in a shop.

While he was eating, he tried to think; but all the normal processes of thought seemed to be blocked.

Reluctantly, he put down his knife and fork and gave his attention to Liz. The pistol was still pointing steadily at him. "Chances are I could kick the table over and snatch the pistol," he thought. "She'd be too surprised to shoot."

But he didn't kick the table over or attempt to do anything. He was saddened by the pistol. He was saddened by Liz. He was saddened by the sudden inescapable knowledge that his tiny island was no longer big enough.

"Jane?" he asked unemotionally.

"Jane," confirmed Liz.

"How long have we been together? It seems quite a long time."

Liz thought for a moment. "Three months, I suppose . . . You lose track."

"Four months," corrected Greville. "Four months and about two weeks. The way things are, it's practically a lifetime."

"It's over," said Liz flatly. "It was nice, but it's over. I'm going to look for Jane. I should have gone a long time ago. You shouldn't have stopped me. That way we'd have still remembered the happiness."

"I love you," said Greville. "That means something?"

"Yes." She hesitated. "But not enough."

"I saved you from the dogs."

"I'm glad about that." She smiled impishly. "But you also saved yourself, didn't you?"

"From the dogs?"

"No. From dying . . . It's no good. I've made up my mind. I'm going. I've got to find Jane or I shan't get any peace."

Greville surveyed her sombrely. "I'll tell you something. I'm not sure I believe in Jane."

Liz tightened her grip on the pistol. Her knuckle showed white where her finger had taken the first pressure on the trigger. "What the hell do you mean?"

"I'm not sure I believe in Jane," repeated Greville

calmly. "I think she may be a figment of your warped imagination. I think she may be nothing more than an excuse for you to do whatever comes into your little transie mind. I think she may be a carefully cooked up excuse that you've given yourself for continuing to stay alive."

For a moment or two, he thought she was going to shoot him; then suddenly she began to laugh. It was high, hysterical laughter. The kind of laughter, thought Greville, that you might indulge in if you were shocked, hurt or afraid.

"You big, stupid bastard," said Liz. "Do you think I could spend months needling myself with nightmares about somebody who doesn't exist?"

"Yes. We're all slightly nuts or we wouldn't be here. It may suit you to have an imaginary sister. For all I know, you may have a bloody great dose of schizophrenia. Jane could be your private piece of therapy —enduring all possible ills and degradation just because you feel guilty because you are still alive. Maybe you even had a twin sister. Maybe she died. What proof have you got that you're not just playing psychological games?"

"I don't need to prove anything to anybody," said Liz simply. "Jane is real enough for me. That's all that matters. And I've got to find her ... You remember that morning on Chelsea Bridge? Hell, you don't think I was taking risks like that just for kicks, do you?"

"Why not?" retorted Greville. "I had a damn silly reason myself for being on Chelsea Bridge. Why shouldn't you be just as crazy as I am?"

Liz laughed. "This is getting us nowhere. The only problem to be solved is whether I have to put a bullet in you or whether I go peacefully ... You can stop me, as I said. But then there'd be a next time; and I wouldn't let you stop me then."

Greville looked at her and thought of all the good times they had had, remembering the love-makings, the insatiable appetite for music, the shared dangers and discoveries.

"Where is this alleged Jane?" he asked at length. "Did your nightmares, imaginings or whatever give you a convenient map reference?"

"She's in a kind of brothel near Manchester," answered Liz evenly. "It's a kind of cellar—I think it's underneath a town hall, or something like that. They keep her in a cage, and she gets screwed about four times a day, and if she's lucky she gets just about enough to eat. But they never let her out of the cellar. She doesn't know whether it's summer or winter. She thinks she's been there about a million years . . . She's ill."

"That's bloody marvellous," exploded Greville. "Assuming it's not all a product of your sick mind, what do you expect to do—home in on the psychic emanations like a guided missile? And even if you do that, what the hell can you do when you get there? Shoot up the place single-handed? God dammit! If you want to commit suicide, why don't you just walk into the lake?"

"Thanks for the encouragement. If there's nothing else to be done, at least I can join her. That way we'll share the load . . . Now, if you haven't got any further illuminating observations, I'll get my bits and pieces together—assuming, of course, you prefer not to be shot first. I'll need the car, I think. But you shouldn't have much difficulty picking up another one that still works . . . So the only question that remains to be answered is whether I pull the trigger or not."

"You crazy little bitch," said Greville quietly. "You bloody little screwing machine." He got up from the table, turned his back on her and walked through the doorway.

"Where do you think you're going?" snapped Liz.

"To look for a bleeding map," he called over his shoulder. "I've got one somewhere. If we're going to bust up the happy home and go to Manchester—which is one of the most elaborate ways of dying that I can think of—then we'll need to choose a route that combines the maximum safety with the maximum speed. To think I've been hoarding petrol for a half-cock trip like this!"

Liz stared after him, wide-eyed. Then she dropped the pistol and began to cry. Greville pretended to take no notice. He found the map—an ancient Esso road map, badly torn and with two sections missing—and spread it over the bed. Then he found a pencil and began to draw an intricate series of lines that criss-crossed the trunk-roads and avoided all towns.

He was still absorbed in plotting a route that would add up to less than two hundred miles—he had cautiously allowed twenty-five miles to the gallon—when Liz followed him into the bedroom.

She had discarded the pistol. She had also discarded her clothes. She was shivering a little. She lifted the map off the still unmade bed and scrambled between the sheets.

"I haven't got anything else," she said with a grin. "Besides, what else can you expect from a screwing machine?"

Greville began to take his shirt off. "We'll start tomorrow morning," he said, "early. I don't much care whether Jane is real or not. I don't much care whether we get to Manchester or not. But I'll do my best ... One way or another, it had to come."

"Yes," murmured Liz. "It had to come."

Oddly enough, and despite the promptings of sheer physical desire, they did not make love. There were too many ghosts. There was Jane and there was Francis. And above all, there was the sadly overwhelming ghost of a tiny refuge that was about to cease to exist.

Until this moment, thought Greville, he had never properly appreciated his cottage on the island at Ambergreave. It was the only place where he had learned what it was to be alive. It was the only place he had ever loved because it was the only place where he had dared to place his entire self in bondage.

He lay there with Liz in his arms, touching her for the sheer delight of touching. It didn't matter that Francis and Jane were standing at the foot of the bed. It didn't matter that mankind had gone down the drain and that personal death was lurking round the corner.

It mattered only that two people could come close enough to look at each other and, though they could never really touch each other or understand each other, not be afraid. Man, he reflected, was doomed to perpetual loneliness though he had never been programmed for it. Man—every man—was a skilled impersonator. But just occasionally there was no need to impersonate anyone or anything. It was enough to exist.

He looked at Liz, lying quietly by his side, and felt as if he were seeing her for the first and last time. He looked at the subtle curves of her breasts, the enigmatic roundness of her belly, the small brown forest that grew between her legs.

Here, he thought, is life. Here is the ancient song. Here is the non-verbal answer to all the verbal sophistications that men have used to demolish themselves and each other since time began.

Then he looked through the window at the grey November light, at the motionless leaves rimmed with a myriad crystals, at the sleeping branches of the apple trees, and back again to the sad long light of impunity.

He didn't want to make love. He just wanted to hold close and pray.

The only trouble was he was too proud, too empty and too lonely for prayer.

## TWENTY-THREE

It had taken them the best part of three days to get within ten miles of Leicester. Greville had optimistically calculated that they could get to Leicester, which was slightly past the half-way mark, with about a hundred and twenty miles of driving. Instead, it had taken nearly two hundred miles of driving; and at that rate, unless he could indulge in a bit of successful scrounging, he would only have enough petrol for a one-way journey. But probably, he reflected with bitter consolation, it was only going to be a one-way journey, anyway. What Liz hoped to accomplish when and if they got as far as Manchester, he had no idea. It was a crazy expedition undertaken for the craziest of reasons in a crazy world by two crazy people. Its chances of success —even if success were only to be defined as mere survival—were just about zero.

They had made a late start from Ambergreave, for there was more work to be done than he had thought. They might have made an earlier start if Liz had not spent half the night screaming. The nightmares had begun a little after midnight. When the screaming started, he had slapped her; but she didn't even open her eyes. It was as if she were in a trance, lost without recall in the terrors of a private world. The first fit didn't last much more than an hour. When Liz came out of it, she refused to talk. She just looked at him, wild-eyed, as if he were a total stranger. Greville got up and made a warm drink for them both. Then they got a little sleep—until the next session. That didn't last quite so long; but there were two more bursts of the same trance-like hysteria before dawn; and when they finally got up they were both bleary-eyed and already worn out.

After a hurried and rather sumptuous breakfast—they had far more food than they could take with them on the journey—Greville had rowed ashore and checked the car, while Liz busied herself collecting guns, ammunition and provisions.

There had been a hard frost and the windows of the station wagon were iced up. It took Greville the best part of an hour to clear them, check the tyres, oil, petrol and battery, and get the engine warmed up. At first he thought it wasn't going to start—the battery didn't seem to have enough juice in it to turn the engine over. Eventually, after about twenty minutes of cranking, he managed to get it to fire. He raced it for a while until the whole engine was warm, then switched off and rowed back to the island.

Liz had got most of their treasures out of the cellar and had dumped them in a pile on the floor. There was far too much to carry, and more time was lost over the selection process.

By the time they were ready to move, both of them were feeling hungry again; so they sat down amid the wreckage of their little citadel to eat a final meal.

Greville surveyed what had been his private, secure and very comfortable retreat gloomily. Once it had felt and looked like home. He didn't think he would ever see it again. Whatever else happened on the fantastic expedition which they were about to undertake, he did not think there would ever be any absolute turning back. The shade of Augustus Rowley could now rest in peace—until the next plague of locusts.

By the time they eventually got started, a red, wintry sun was peeping through the cloud-laden sky. To Greville, it seemed to be the colour of blood—a discouraging omen. Nevertheless, he gave Liz a cheery grin and started the car. They were on their way.

Then everything began to go wrong. Greville had not realised how rapidly the world in which he lived was deteriorating. Two of the roads he had chosen for the first day's run were blocked—one by a large tree that had fallen across it, and the other by a large hole so camouflaged by grass and weeds that he nearly drove into it.

Greville was impressed by the hole. He got out of the car and inspected it. The grass that covered it had the air of grass that had been established for quite a long time: the dead and dying weeds—convolvulus, nettles, groundsel and bistort—looked as if they had been there since the beginning of the world. He came to the conclusion that the hole had been caused by high explosive. Quite a lot of it. He wondered why such a quiet country lane should have received such attention. He was wondering about it for a long time. But after a couple of days of hard driving, during which he had encountered several such holes, he thought he had the answer.

The roads he had chosen led only through small villages; and if anyone still lived in those villages they might reasonably be expected to protect themselves as best they could against scroungers—particularly well-armed and motorised scroungers, and most particularly against scroungers in convoy who might be able to overwhelm any local resistance and take whatever they wanted.

Greville had a sudden mental vision of all the roads of England—why stop at England? All the roads of the world—being steadily choked by weeds and grass and trees or being deliberately destroyed by man. In the end, with radio and telephone gone, with travel reduced to what a man could accomplish by walking, the world would contain nothing but groups of desert islanders. Strangers would be feared not because they might be dangerous but simply because they were strangers. Then tabu would raise its indestructible head once more; and anyone who did not belong to the family, sect, clan or tribe would be destroyed for the very clear and logical reason that he did not belong.

Greville had to make two major and several minor detours before darkness on the first day. When darkness came, he tried driving on his headlamps; but the effort was too tiring. There was always the risk that every clump of grass concealed a hazard, and even if it was only a pot-hole large enough to break a half-shaft, it was still large enough not only to wreck the expedition but to completely ruin the chances of its survival. For Greville and Liz were already a long way from any known sanctuary; and while it was still possible to attempt to get back to Ambergreave on foot, the possibility was not such as to inspire optimism.

They drove off the road and spent the first night in a little clearing that had once been part of a large field. Liz had brought a paraffin stove; and so they were able to heat some of their tinned food and have a reasonably satisfying meal.

They slept uneasily and uncomfortably in the car with the windows up. It was just as well that Greville, despite protestations from Liz, had refused to allow any ventilation.

Huddled together in contortions which they would regret bitterly next day, they had not been dozing long when there was a pattering all over the car that sounded like heavy rainfall. However, it was not heavy rainfall, as Greville discovered when he switched on the interior lighting. It was rats—hundreds or more probably thousands of them—trying to get in.

They could smell meat; and the meat they could smell was filled with terror. Liz gazed at the phalanx of vicious little faces on the bonnet and began to shake uncontrollably. With a curse, Greville leaned forward and pressed the horn. The rats disappeared almost instantly; but within a second or two they were back.

Greville switched on the headlights and illuminated an entire mobile carpet of rats. The clearing was alive with them. They seemed to ebb and flow, an evil hungry tide that looked as if it was about to engulf the entire car.

He started the engine. The noise drove them back briefly. But they became accustomed to it and came on once more.

In a fit equally compounded of anger and fear and plain irritability, Greville slipped the car into first gear and began to drive round the clearing in a tight circle. The rats fell away from the bonnet. Those already on the roof were thrown clear by the motion. Dozens of them, hypnotised by the headlights, passed beneath the wheels. They were immediately torn to pieces by those who perished next time round.

Eventually, it dawned upon the rats that they were on a no-win basis. The survivors—and that included the vast majority—took their leave. But they left behind them a stench; and the stench was so bad that Greville had to move the car back to the relatively exposed road.

Again they tried to settle down to sleep; but sleep would not come. And it was with relief that they took up the journey once more at first light.

It was another jewelled morning. The flat East Anglian landscape, unfettered now, free from the tidy patterns of agriculture, the greedy attentions of man, was reverting to its own primal mystery. Fen and woodland marched towards each other; and the rolling brown acres of ploughed land were no more.

The frost was a heavy one; but the car started easily. While it was warming up Greville and Liz stretched themselves and stamped about to get warm. Liz wanted to make a hot drink, but Greville decided to drive for a while first. As far as human beings—and animals—were concerned, early morning was probably a good time for travelling. Very few of either were at their aggressive best until the day had properly started. Frost translated the petrified landscape into the kind of pictures that were used to illustrate old-fashioned children's books. Any moment, thought Greville as he chugged along cautiously at twenty-five miles an hour, one might be confronted by the inevitable knight on a white charger. Or possibly dragons.

But neither knights nor dragons presumed to materialise in the desolate, white-edged world. He and Liz were alone with a car-load of junk and desperation.

They were driving from nowhere to nowhere, from oblivion to oblivion, through frozen avenues of time on a winter morning that any sensitive person would have recognised as the naked manifestation of eternity.

In a couple of hours, they had covered nearly thirty miles, which, allowing for the usual stops, map consultations (virtually useless because sign-posts were more or less non-existent) and three small detours, was pretty good going.

Greville felt pleased with himself. He felt entitled to enjoy his breakfast. It consisted of eggs and home-made bread and some precious coffee. Taken by the roadside, with the eggs cooked in bacon fat and the bread used to polish the pan clean and the black coffee stinging his throat like some deliciously painful nectar, he could almost feel happy. He looked at Liz, and his spirits rose. Whatever happened, he told himself firmly, they would stay together.

During the rest of the day they made good progress. Huntingdon had been by-passed without incident. There remained Kettering and Market Harborough as the only towns of appreciable size before Leicester. If he exercised a little bit of ingenuity, it should be possible to get round both of them without too much difficulty.

But whatever route was taken, they could not avoid villages. The two that they passed through during the morning were as silent as the grave. No smoke rose from the chimney-stacks. Cottage windows, glassless, stared blank-eyed and mute. In the third village, passed shortly after midday, a pack of dogs seemed to have used the houses as a temporary refuge. At the sound of the car they came hurling out of doorways and even first-storey windows, eager for something to kill and eat. Watching them lunge futilely at the wheels and the bodywork, Greville was almost sorry for the half-starved brutes. After all, they had been deserted by those to whom traditionally they were supposed to be the best of friends; and like man, they just didn't know what had hit them.

A more pleasing sight occurred later in the afternoon when Liz and Greville caught sight of a huge herd of deer. They were passing through relatively open country at the time; and the herd of deer were bounding across the plain—almost parallel with the road—in joyous exultation, glorying in life, freedom, the sharp air of late autumn, and the marvellous absence of the restraining and frequently lethal hand of man.

Being of a practical turn of mind, Liz suggested that they stop the car and drop one of the deer for meat. Greville vetoed the idea. He said he didn't want to waste time skinning and cutting; but secretly he was too moved by the obvious *joie de vivre* of the herd to want to do anything to spoil it. Besides, they had plenty of food for the time being. The time to shoot deer was when one really needed to.

They had covered nearly seventy miles by nightfall. It wasn't a bad start. It wasn't bad at all. This time Greville chose a small hill on which to spend the night—a hill that, according to the map, was miles from anywhere. He kept the car on the roadside, partly on the theory that any predatory animals would be more likely to haunt the nearby woodland and partly on the theory that it would be easier to move away if he had to.

There were no incidents, however—at least, none apart from Liz. The nightmares seemed to be taking an even tighter hold on her. She did not scream this time, she just moaned and shivered and cried softly. Nothing Greville could do would rouse her; and she remained curled up in her seat, sleeping at times, but for most of the time emitting sad and inhuman little noises until well after daybreak.

When, at last, she came to her senses, she did not seem to recognise Greville for a time; and she was strangely uncommunicative throughout most of the morning. She had cooked breakfast like an automaton, programmed for the task. And, in the same way, she had eaten it.

Greville humoured her and tried not to intrude too much upon her private thoughts. It seemed to him that as the morning wore on her spirits were raised slightly. He assumed it was because they were near to Leicester and because she felt that the worst part of the journey was behind them.

But it had nothing to do with how far they were from Leicester or Manchester.

While they were driving along a monotonously straight and relatively clear piece of roadway, Liz said abruptly: "Jane's dead. She died last night ... I'm going to have a baby."

Greville stopped the car and gazed at her in wonderment. "Say it all again—slowly. Maybe I'm further round than I thought."

"Jane's dead," repeated Liz. "She died last night. It was some kind of fever ... Hell, I don't really know what it was. Maybe it was just starvation and misery, or maybe she just couldn't stand the screwing any more ... Anyway, she said to thank you. She said you were all right ... So now we don't need to go to Manchester any more, do we? She really is dead, you know ... I've been ... I've been cut off. It's an odd sensation ... A long time ago I read in a book somewhere about people that had to have limbs amputated. Afterwards, some of them could still feel the fingers and arms that weren't there ... Phantom limbs, I think they were called ... Now I've got a phantom limb ... It's funny, really."

Greville looked at her. She was dry-eyed and almost abnormally calm. There was not even a tremor in her voice.

"So Jane's dead," he managed to say finally. "I'm sorry ... I really am sorry ... You're sure she's dead?"

"I'm sure."

Greville was silent for a minute or two. "You said something else," he prompted at length. "It didn't seem to be connected with Jane."

"That's right. I'm going to have a baby."

He was silent again for a while. Then: "How long have you known?"

"Three months," said Liz unconcernedly. "Maybe four ... You begin to lose track of time."

"And why the bloody hell didn't you tell me before?" he exploded violently.

Liz smiled. "It will be a little girl ... I expect I shall call her Jane."

"I said why the hell didn't you tell me before?"

"You might have chucked me out. You might have told me to go and have my bloody baby in a field ...

Besides, you should have known. You saw I was getting fatter, didn't you?"

"You were skin and bone when I found you. I thought you were just putting on weight because you were eating reasonably well for a change."

Liz laughed. "That's a good one! It's the best excuse for blindness I've heard yet."

"Why didn't you tell me!" he raged.

"Because," she said quietly, "I don't even know if you are the father. It could be one of the Richmond Lot. It could be one of the Northerners. It could even be one of those wretched kids that screwed me on the way out of London ... I was afraid to tell you. But now I'm not afraid any more, because I know that everything is going to be all right ... It will be a little girl and I shall call her Jane."

Greville stared at her helplessly. He felt as if someone had just hit him with a block of wood—about fifteen times.

"Let's try to get some grip on reality," he said in a carefully controlled voice. "Always assuming, of course, that there's a bit of reality to get a grip on ... You say Jane's dead. All right, I accept that. I was never sure she was alive, so I can't much quibble about her dying ... But this baby ... Goddammit, you can't be that woolly-headed. You must have some idea."

"No idea," retorted Liz flatly. "That time I ran away —it wasn't just for Jane, you know. I thought I'd find her and then we could go somewhere quiet and then I could have my baby, and you never need know ... I've got to say this. I can't really care who the father is." She patted her stomach protectively. "After all, she's mine."

"Jesus Christ!" said Greville helplessly. "What in the world do we do now?"

Liz seemed to be in command of the situation. "Turn back," she said. "We'll go back to the cottage and you can screw me as much as you like—except for a little time before baby comes and a little time afterwards ... Then we shall all be happy."

"Shall we indeed," snapped Greville. "Shall we indeed!"

He raced the car's engine, went into first gear viciously and tore away with a jerk. Throwing caution to the winds, he began to cruise along at nearly forty miles an hour, his spirit numbed, oblivious of everything. The road began to twist and turn, but he did not slow down.

He did not see the sign: *Beware trespassers. You are approaching manorial territory.* It was a big sign, newly painted, at the side of the road. But he didn't see it.

He didn't even see the road-block until it was too late. Anyway, it was a damn silly road-block—a few bales of hay manned (if that was the right word) by a couple of tweedy-looking gents with shot-guns.

Seeing that he had left it too late to reverse, he slowed down a little as if he proposed to stop. Then when he was about twenty yards from the bales of hay, he changed down into second gear and accelerated like the devil.

The engine screamed, the gear-box whined, and the station wagon leapt forward, scattering men and bales with reckless abandon. Greville saw one of the men bowled head over heels, his shot-gun going off as it pointed to the sky. It gave him a savage delight. He hoped the man was hurt—badly hurt. He hoped he would live quite a long time to nurse his pain.

The other man had disappeared completely from view, but he was evidently shooting, for the car was rattling as if it had been hit by a volley of hail-stones. Then they were through the tumbling barrier of bales and away.

Greville gave a cry of triumph. The road-block had occurred at a good time. It had occurred when he badly needed to do something and smash somebody.

He was still accelerating, still filled with a bubbling boiling mixture of anger and violence and hatred and love when suddenly there was a sound like the end of the world. The roadway seemed to drift up towards him in slow motion like a snapped ribbon. Then the car slewed over sideways and began to roll.

The last thing he heard was Liz shouting.

The last word he heard was: "Jane!"

Then suddenly, inexplicably, there was nothing but fog. And the fog became a black enveloping river.

## TWENTY-FOUR

THERE was a cage. He couldn't get in, and Liz couldn't get out. She was naked, and she wasn't alone in the cage. There was a ring of male faces. Greedy faces, vacant faces—slack with lust and anticipation.

Francis stood by Greville's side, dressed like a circus ring-master. "Walk up! Walk up!" he shouted jovially. "See the greatest little show on earth. See the beautiful lady ridden bareback by the most intrepid erection and demolition experts in the world . . . Walk up! Walk up!"

"Stop!" screamed Greville, his voice making no sound. "That's Liz. You can't let them do that to Liz."

"Walk up! Walk up!" said Francis, oblivious. "See the *Turn of the Screw* in three dimensions and natural colour."

Big Ears was in the cage. "Let's have a go," he pleaded. "There's nothing else to do."

Nibs was also present. "By all means," he said grandly, "provided you repent afterwards of such sordid fornication. Let us trust this is a lesson to poor Uncle. I am afraid that at times he harbours indelicate thoughts."

"Stop it!" screamed Greville silently. "She's mine. Liz belongs to me."

Francis took off his top-hat and put on a mortar-board and gown. "Gentlemen," he said, "we have here a most interesting example of paranoia. The patient has delusions of considerable grandeur. Note the simple phrasing: Liz belongs to me. Apparently, gentlemen, the patient genuinely believes that he is capable of possessing another human being. Extrapolating further, I think it is only fair to adduce his belief in the concept of romantic love."

"I love her," said Grenville mechanically. "She belongs to me."

"Go stuff yourself," retorted Smiler.

Francis dissolved into Father Jack. He regarded Greville benevolently. "*Ego te absolvo*, my son."

Liz waved at Greville cheerily. "I'm no good at anything but screwing," she said.

Father Jack shot her neatly through the forehead.

And Greville woke up screaming.

"Steady, lad! Steady there! You're with friends."

The room came into focus; and with it a man's face. It was large, round and ruddy. It had a thick, grey moustache and on top a thin, receding line of hair. The lips were smiling but the eyes were cold and remote. The head was attached to a body. The body wore a check shirt and a tweed jacket.

Greville stopped screaming. "Where's Liz?" The words were no more than an exhausted whisper.

"Ah yes, the woman." Cold Eyes paused. "It's no good beating about the bush, laddie. Take it on the chin, there's a good fellow. Best in the end, what? She's dead, d'you know."

"Dead?" Greville felt suddenly numb.

"Dead," repeated Cold Eyes. "Mean to say: you can't go driving cars all over land-mines without making a bit of an omelette, what?"

"Dead," repeated Greville stupidly. "Dead."

"After all," went on Cold Eyes. "It was a bit naughty, wasn't it? My men asked you very decently to heave to. But off you go like a mad thing without so much as a civil 'by your leave'. It's a wonder you aren't dead, too, laddie. The car is pretty much a write-off." He laughed heartily. "Still, what the hell. There's no need to worry about your no-claim bonus, eh? Main thing is to get you up and about ... No bones broken. Would you believe it! The devil takes care of his own."

"Who—who are you?" asked Greville.

"Name of Oldknow, laddie. Sir James Oldknow—not that it matters these days ... My boys seem to like to call me Squire."

"Where the hell am I?"

"Ah, the classic question," said Cold Eyes jovially. "You are in Brabyns House, laddie, in the village of Upper Brabyns, in the manor of Brabyns, Leicestershire ... And now it's my turn. What's your name?"

"Greville."

"Christian or Surname?"

"Both."

"Don't play games, laddie. I'm a busy man." Cold Eyes made a sign, and another face came into Greville's field of vision. It was attached to a massive body.

The newcomer slapped Greville's face twice—hard. As he tried to avoid the second blow, he realised that he was in a bed.

"Be good," said the burly man, "and answer the Squire's questions. He doesn't like people who don't co-operate."

"Now," said Sir James Oldknow. "Christian or Surname?"

"Surname."

"And your Christian name is—?"

"Matthew."

Sir James smiled once more with his lips only. "How nice. We already have Mark, Luke and John . . . How old are you?"

Greville had to think about that one. "Thirty-seven."

"You look ten years older . . . The white hair, I suppose."

"I feel ten years older."

The burly one slapped him again. "The Squire doesn't like cheekiness," he said.

"What was your profession?" asked Sir James.

"Grave-digger."

"Naughty," said Sir James. "Very naughty." He gave a sign, and the burly man advanced on Greville once more.

"You're a slow learner." The burly man hit Greville in the throat. He was too weak to avoid the blow. Sir James waited patiently until he had finished coughing and gasping.

"Profession?" he repeated. "That is, before the solar eruptions, of course."

"Adman."

"I beg your pardon."

"Advertising man . . . I was a copywriter."

"Splendid," said Sir James, rubbing his hands. "Absolutely splendid. I have just the job for you. In a way, I suppose it's promotion . . . No doubt you will be happy to learn, Mr. Greville, that you will shortly enter the field of Public Relations."

Greville felt a hysterical urge to laugh bubbling dangerously inside him. He fought it down. Sir James Oldknow did not look as if he would approve of laughter—unless it was his own.

"Public Relations?" echoed Greville blankly.

"You heard me the first time, laddie. Try to keep a grip on things. It'll be an advantage—to you . . . Now, are you going to take a sensible interest in life?"

"Yes." The burly man was out of sight once more, but not out of mind.

"Then I'll put you in the picture." Sir James Oldknow settled himself on the side of the bed. "My family has had a few thousand acres in this part of the world for about three centuries . . . Not that that's important in itself, d'you know. But it gives a man roots. It gives him his bearings . . . D'you see what I'm driving at?"

"I think so."

"Well, now. Here I am in this topsy-turvy world, a man with land, a knowledge of how to deal with men, a sense of position and—though I say it myself—a bit of a flair for leadership . . . It begins to add up, doesn't it?"

"Yes," agreed Greville carefully, "it begins to add up."

"The point is," continued Sir James, "when the sun gets a bit off-colour and people start kicking the bucket, it makes for a nasty spot of anarchy—unless you're lucky enough to have somebody who knows what's what."

"I imagine you know what's what," supplied Greville.

"That's it, laddie, that's it. I know what's what . . . Incidentally, while I think of it, have you got any Negro blood in you?"

The impulse to laughter bubbled once more, but Greville managed to suppress it. "I don't think so."

"Good. Good . . . You don't look as if you have. But what about Jewish blood? That's a bit more insidious, isn't it?"

"I'm afraid I haven't got any Jewish blood either. Is that bad?"

"No, laddie. It's excellent. Depending on how you shape, I might even consider you for breeding purposes. We're a bit thin on intellectuals . . . Now where was I?"

"What's what," prompted Greville.

"Ah, yes. Well, that's me. The point is, laddie, I represent order in chaos. Stability. Permanence. Some chap once wrote about the rich enduring qualities of the English tradition. Well, there you have it. You see, with the world as it is we've got to take a sensible approach. And that brings us back to the feudal system, doesn't it?"

"Inescapably," agreed Greville. Soon, he was thinking, soon I shall be able to cry for Liz. If I humour him, maybe this clown will go away; and then I shall be able to think about her. I shall be able to build up a picture of what she was like. I shall be able to see the look on her face when I kissed her—and the look there was when she told me about the child ... Oh, Liz! Dear, warm Liz!

"Basically," said Sir James, "it's a mutual security pact. I look after you: you look after me. You swear fealty: I swear to protect you. Damn simple. Damn fine arrangement. I've got two hundred and forty-seven men, seventy-four women and about two thousand acres. You've got yourself. We strike a bargain. You give me energy and loyalty. I give you security and protection. What could be neater?"

"Nothing at all," said Greville tactfully. "Nothing at all."

"Good. Then you're in the Public Relations business ... Very properly, my people are a bit afraid of me. That's good. That's very good. But it's important that they should understand me—that's where you come in. And when they understand me, it's important that they should like me—that's where you come in again ... I'm a bluff old type. No finesse. Never had time for it. That's where you come in once more. Understanding, liking, finesse. Your department. People have to know that what I tell 'em to do is for their own good ... Now, how does it sound to you?"

"A definite challenge," said Greville.

"Think you can meet the challenge?"

"I hope so."

"Good. There'll be speeches, news sheets—that sort of thing. You see, I want my people psychologically prepared for war."

Greville was weak and aching, and he was beginning to feel light-headed. "For war?" he repeated dully.

"For war," said Sir James emphatically. "The age-old struggle has never been—as friend Marx would have us believe—between the haves and the have-nots. That was just a damn big socialist-communist red herring. The real struggle is between order and anarchy. Order as represented by established authority, and anarchy as represented by the long-haired decadents who gibber about equality and all that rot . . . Point of fact, there's a rather nasty bunch of annies about five miles away. Their presence is, to say the least, disturbing. Not only do they give sanctuary to a few of my runaway serfs—in every society there are bound to be a few malcontents—but they attempt to undermine me with subversive propaganda. Incidentally, that'll be another of your jobs—counter-propaganda . . . Anyway, as I see it, the trick is to deal with the annies before they outnumber us . . . So my people have got to be made to see what a rotten lot of decadent bastards they are. D'you follow me?"

Greville's head was aching, his limbs were aching and his throat was aching. More than anything he wanted to be alone. "The lucidity of your argument is admirable, Sir James," he said. "You may count on me to do whatever I can." For a sickening moment, he was afraid he had overplayed it. In fact, he knew he had overplayed it. But Sir James Oldknow was impervious to irony.

"Splendid," he said. "Absolutely splendid. Tomorrow we must get you out of bed. Then you can have the regulation two weeks' basic training, and then you shall swear the oath of fealty. After that, my dear fellow, you're in business. Do a good job and you will not find me ungrateful."

"What is the basic training about?"

"Oh, lots of things," said Sir James, airily. "Husbandry, unarmed combat, the use of the longbow."

"I see . . . I'm already a pretty fair shot with a rifle."

Sir James Oldknow laughed. "Firearms," he said, "are strictly for the use of the Praetorian guard . . . You have quite a lot to learn, laddie. I hope you benefit by it."

# TWENTY-FIVE

It was nine days before Greville managed to make his escape from Sir James Oldknow and his latter-day feudal system. But for two men—known respectively as Nosey and Big Tom—he might not have attempted to escape at all, or, at least, not until it was too late; for he was haunted by memories of Liz. The thought that he would never see her again sapped his energy and even his self-respect. For a while he was not really sure whether he wanted to live or die. Memories of Chelsea Bridge rose disturbingly in his mind—not of the day when he saved Liz from the dogs but of the night he killed Pauline.

He had killed her, he thought, because he was trying to kill himself. Maybe he had killed Liz for the same reason and, oddly, in a similar way. Maybe both episodes constituted one of the odd little jokes of history. Maybe the possibility that someone else's child lay cradled in Liz's belly was somehow a sequel to the fact that other men than he had lain between Pauline's legs. And maybe Liz and Pauline were the same person in a different world . . .

Fortunately he didn't have much time for introspection. Come to that, he didn't have much time for anything. Sir James Oldknow was as good as his word. Weak though he was, Greville was hauled out of his bed early on the following day by Big Tom—the heavy individual who had been present at his interview with Sir James.

It was barely after dawn when Big Tom arrived. Greville was still uneasily asleep. Big Tom picked him up like a child and set him on his feet. Then he threw his clothes at him.

"The Squire says for you to get basic training," he announced happily. "I'm basic training." He laughed. "By the time I've finished with you, you'll think there's nothing more basic in the world. I'm going to toughen you up. Even a bloody clerk has to be able to stand on his own two feet."

After he had dressed, Greville was taken out of Brabyns House, through two wooden gates in two wire fences that he later learned were electrified, and to a kind of mess hall where about twenty men were eating breakfast.

Breakfast consisted of porridge, some rather grey bread, a slice of bacon and a hot drink that was obviously meant to be a coffee substitute and tasted like burnt toast mixed with water. Greville was allowed ten minutes for eating; then training began.

Along with the other men, whom Big Tom was attempting to forge into a commando unit for the coming war against the annies, Greville was put through all the acute miseries of an assault course. He was too weak to resist. In fact he was still too weak even to last out the morning. After physical exercises, there was archery and knifemanship; and after that there were more exercises. Greville collapsed long before the midday break. Big Tom had a bucket of water thrown over him, then he was carried to a large wooden hut with straw-filled mattresses on the floor and left there to dry off and meditate. He was too exhausted to do either. He fell asleep wet and woke up wet and shivering.

It was almost dark and somebody was shaking him. It was a man who introduced himself as Nosey.

"Wake up, mate," said Nosey. "I've got a ration of stew here for you. Better get it down. There's nowt else till tomorrow."

The stew was in an old tin can. It smelt nauseating; but Greville was suddenly and dreadfully hungry.

"Stewed cat," said Nosey. "It's better than dog—more like rabbit. Except that the bleeding cook doesn't know what to do with decent meat ... Here, I've got a bit of news for you. She's alive."

"Alive?" repeated Greville blankly.

"Your old woman, mate. The Squire had her put in the pen—that's the place where he keeps women that are not for the likes of you and me ... She's got a duck in the oven, I hear. So nobody gets her until she's foaled down. The Squire's very proper about things like that."

During the ten minutes or so that passed before the rest of the men returned to the barracks, Greville learned quite a lot about the Squire and his little community. But the thought that dominated him was that Liz was still alive. It was an elixir. It seemed to pump the will to live back into his veins.

When the other men came, Nosey immediately switched his conversation to obviously safe subjects—food, women and Big Tom. Food and women, it appeared, were strictly rationed. Big Tom, on the other hand, was completely unrationed. He was also universally disliked. Not hated, just disliked. For though he had fought and beaten every man in the barracks—it was all part of the basic training—he had enough sense to be magnanimous in victory. He respected men who could fight well; and anyone who was fortunate enough to give almost as good as he got could be sure of the occasional extra ration of both food and sex. Big Tom could lift a hundredweight sack of corn in each hand simultaneously. He offered every recruit the choice of fighting him or lifting the corn. If they chose to lift the corn and failed he would beat them until they were unconscious. Big Tom was a third-generation Liverpool-Irishman. He was also a devout Catholic. The Squire had given him a woman, and he had given the woman three children. Every Sunday he walked with her to Brabyns Church where the Squire, also a Catholic, officiated as part-time priest.

Conversation in the barracks was of brief duration, for the men were tired out. Nosey took a palliasse next to Greville's. Presently they were both surrounded by snores and heavy breathing. But Nosey remained awake.

"Hey, Greville," he whispered at length. "Think you'll stick it?"

"Stick what?"

"This here feudal lark. The Squire's dead keen on it. Gives us history lessons. Says we've got to go backwards before we can go forwards ... Maybe he's got something. But I shouldn't like to be one of his villains, or whatever he calls 'em. He has 'em branded, you know. A big V stuck right in the middle of the forehead. Keeps 'em in the old stables ... Mind you he only makes villains out of blokes that give a bit of sauce ... Think you'll stick it?"

"No," said Greville. "I don't think I'll stick it. I think I'll get my girl back and take off."

Nosey smothered a laugh. "You'll be lucky. You'll be bloody lucky, mate. The Squire may be a bit weak in his nut, but he's got this whole place sown up tight . . . The last bloke that tried it was hunted down like a fox . . . Tally-ho, and all that. The old Squire still keeps a pack of hounds. Would you believe it—dogs all over the damn country, and he keeps a pack of hounds . . . They made a right mess of this bloke I'm telling you about. All that was left was his shoes."

"Then why the hell did you ask me whether I was going to stick it?" demanded Greville irritably.

Nosey laughed quietly. " 'Cos I ain't going to stick it, neither, mate. My old bag wasn't much, but he didn't have no call to put her in the bawdy house."

Greville remained silent.

"Know why he put her in the bawdy house?" demanded Nosey rhetorically. " 'Cos she wouldn't wash his bleeding feet . . . Anyway, sleep on it mate—and thank some bastard or other that you ain't dead yet."

"I'll sleep on it," agreed Greville. "Thanks for the stew—and other things."

"Pleasure," whispered Nosey. "Sweet dreams."

Oddly enough, Greville's dreams were extraordinarily sweet. He dreamt about Liz. She was still alive, and that was all that mattered.

The next morning, after a breakfast that was a replica of the previous day's, there was Big Tom and basic training once more. Part of the basic training appeared to consist of felling trees to make a clearing all round what Big Tom called the defence perry-meter. In between spells with seven-pound axes and two-handed saws there were more archery sessions. Greville could not get the hang of the longbow. It made his wrists ache. The arrows either fell short or went gloriously wide. His ineptitude seemed to please Big Tom enormously.

"No wonder you got white hair," he boomed jovially. "You think too much. You're a bloomin' intellectual. Now stop holding the bow like you was trying to play a one-string harp. Fit the arrow, draw it back—and give us a bit of time to get in front of the target, so we'll be safe."

The men rose to Big Tom's unsubtle humour with Pavlovian reflexes. Pretty soon Greville was the butt of the entire group. He accepted the role with equanimity. He felt it might be useful to establish a reputation for being unable to do anything satisfactorily that required skill or sustained physical effort.

The day passed without incident. By the time they returned to the barracks after the evening meal, Greville was worn out. Most of his companions were younger men and had adjusted more easily to the rigorous training. Also none of them had been recently blown up by a land-mine.

Greville felt that his aches and pains were not entirely futile, however. He had acquired quite a knowledge of the topography of the Squire's dominion; and such knowledge was going to come in useful sooner or later.

That night Nosey again found a palliasse that was next to Greville's. "Have you had any bright thoughts yet?" he asked, when it was apparent that the others were asleep.

"Not yet," Greville admitted.

"Not to worry, mate." Nosey chuckled grimly. "We got all the time in the world . . . Me, I'm no good at working out what to do, so you'll have to be the brains. But when you've sorted out what's necessary, I reckon I'll be as useful as the next man."

"We need guns," said Greville, "not bows and arrows."

Nosey laughed. "You'll be lucky. Think again, mate. The only gun you're likely to get near to is the one Big Tom wears—unless the Squire decides he can trust you, or unless they send us out to mop up the annies."

Greville fell asleep trying to devise ways of getting at Big Tom's revolver—not that it would be of much use, because as far as he could make out the rest of the men in his group were sufficiently frightened or sufficiently stupid to be loyal. Some of them were already excellent longbowmen. And whereas a rifle might hold off archers, a revolver was worse than useless.

The next day was pretty much the same as the day before, except that in the afternoon, while he was recovering from a session of unarmed combat, Greville saw a team of six of the Squire's villeins drawing a single-furrow plough. Since the Squire had a number of horses, the sight puzzled him—until Nosey explained that it was a punishment detail. The villeins were supervised by a couple of louts with rifles and truncheons—presumably members of Sir James Oldknow's Praetorian Guard. Greville watched, fascinated, as the men strained to draw the plough through the half-frozen soil. He felt as if the centuries were being stripped away, as if indeed it was possible to make a literal return to the Dark Ages.

Days followed each other. Greville's muscles and spirit toughened. At night, in the blissful few minutes when he was relaxed before sleep came, he thought alternately about Liz—he had already discovered which of the manor house buildings was the pen—and methods of escape. But first, he must find a means of communicating with her. It would be stupid to start anything until he was certain of success. After all, as Nosey had said, there was all the time in the world.

As it turned out, Nosey was wrong. There was very little time left for either of them; and certainly not enough time to establish communications with Liz.

It was on the eighth day of his basic training that Greville was given the choice of lifting two one-hundredweight sacks of corn or fighting Big Tom. In his own peculiar way, Big Tom was fair-minded. He had waited patiently until he judged that Greville was fully recovered. Then he decided to have his bit of fun.

Big Tom was about eighteen stone and Greville was about twelve stone. He chose to lift the corn. Big Tom laughed aloud. He sent two men for the sacks, then lifted them himself and dumped them at Greville's feet. "There you are, me boy. And the saints help you if you can't move the dear little darlings."

Greville had already considered the problem and thought he had an answer. He laid both sacks on their sides, about two feet apart, and pushed most of the corn to the top and the bottom of the sacks, so that each was rather slack in the middle. Then he crouched down, put an arm securely round each sack, and attempted to stand up. He managed to lift both sacks about a foot off the ground before he fell flat on his face.

Some of the group who had been watching applauded, being of the opinion that he had succeeded in the terms of the challenge. But Big Tom was angry. No one else had ever lifted both sacks simultaneously clear of the ground. He felt that Greville had somehow deceived him. He was also determined not to be deprived of his simple pleasure.

"A good try, me boy. But you didn't quite make it." Then to demonstrate what he meant, he hoisted both sacks shoulder high. "So now you'll have to be spanked for being too clever by half."

Whereupon he seized Greville as if he were a child, lifted him horizontally and then dropped him heavily, face down, so that his stomach hit the knee that Big Tom had extended.

Big Tom did not let him go; and while Greville hung there winded and retching, Big Tom brought the flat of his free hand down humiliatingly and heavily on Greville's bottom. The spanking did not last long. It was simply a demonstration of overwhelming superiority.

During the rest of the afternoon, Greville was taciturn and submissive. He wore the aspect of a beaten man—beaten spiritually as well as physically—and because of that Big Tom did not indulge in his customary horseplay. Indeed he seemed to go out of his way to make sure that Greville did not have any strenuous tasks. It was his way of showing that the encounter was past and done with, and that now that Greville knew his place he could be accepted as one of Big Tom's happy family. Oddly enough, a few of the other men were fairly subdued, too. Some of them felt that Big Tom had overdone it. Because Greville's hair was white, they assumed he was quite old; and it seemed to them that Big Tom had deliberately taken advantage of his age.

That night in the barracks men whom Greville did not know by name dropped by to exchange a few words with him. No one mentioned the incident of the sacks of corn; but their very avoidance of the subject made it an unspoken topic for which they were offering unspoken sympathy.

"Don't let it get you," said Nosey, sitting on his palliasse. "From what I can gather, that big bastard didn't do his self no good. He just lost friends and influenced people, like."

"I'm not crying about it, Nosey," remarked Greville evenly. In the dim light he was examining his boots. They were good, solid boots, ex-W.D., with studs in the thick leather soles. "It's all in the day's work."

"You're still going to bust loose?"

"When the time comes." Greville had no idea when the time would come. He was too tired to make plans. He could only hope that after he had done Big Tom's basic training and become the Squire's P.R.O. an opportunity would present itself.

But Greville reckoned without spontaneity, impulse and his own emotions. If anyone had asked him why he was examining his boots in the barracks just before he went to sleep, he could not have given a satisfactory answer. But something deep inside him knew; and something deep inside him was merely waiting for the opportunity.

It came just before midday on the ninth day. Another new recruit had been added to the group—a big, strapping boy of perhaps eighteen. Big Tom had switched his attentions from Greville to the youngster who, becoming bored with his lot as a pig-keeper, had been so rash as to volunteer for special training. He was already regretting the decision; for Big Tom had presented him with the traditional choice, and he had elected to fight. Now he lay on his back, a bruised and bleeding mass, feeling very sorry for himself.

Brief though it was, Greville had watched the fight carefully. Big Tom, he noted, liked to rush in and finish things as quickly as possible. He was an aggressive fighter whose only instinct—fortunately supported by great strength—was to charge and destroy.

Greville chose his position carefully. He was standing on a slight rise in the ground. Then, while Big Tom was preening himself on the easy victory, Greville said in a loud voice: "Nobody but a loud-mouthed overweight idiot could get any glory from beating old men and boys."

Big Tom gazed at him in amazement. "Say that again, me boyo," he grated. "You must be very tired of living."

"Take off that gun," said Greville, glancing at Big

Tom's revolver, "and you'll take off half your courage. Liverpool Irishmen were never much good in a fair match."

Big Tom took the revolver out of its holster. For a moment, Greville thought he had overdone it. For a moment, he thought he was going to collect a bullet for his pains.

But Big Tom laid the revolver carefully down on the grass. "Nobody touch that mind," he warned the now silent group of men who were gazing at Greville in awe. "Nobody touch that. It's going to take me just thirty seconds to break the spine of yon fellow with the sharp tongue—enough time for him to make his peace with God."

Greville did not move. "Your mother must have been a worn-out old cow," he called encouragingly. "You have that sort of face."

With a roar of rage Big Tom charged. Tank-like, he charged up the slight rise at Greville, who waited until he was less than three yards away. Then Greville jumped, drew up his feet, half-twisted sideways and simultaneously straightened both legs as if they had been bent spring steel.

Both boots hit Big Tom full in the face. He catapulted backwards and fell flat on his back with a sickening thud. He did not move.

Greville picked himself up, saw that Nosey had got the revolver, and went to inspect Big Tom. So did one or two of the other men. The rest seemed dazed by the speed of it all.

Big Tom's face was a mess. But that wasn't going to worry him at all. He was dead. In falling, his head had struck a fairly large stone and the stone had smashed his skull.

Someone lifted Big Tom's head, and then there were angry murmurs. But Greville heard Nosey's voice.

"The first man that tries anything gets a bullet in his guts. I've only got six, so that'll leave quite a few of you. But who wants to be one of the six?"

No one answered. Suddenly Greville felt an icy calmness coming over him. It was not working out as he had planned. He had been going to wait; but it was no use waiting now. He had been going to wait until he could get Liz—but now she would have to be abandoned. For a time ... His mind began to work like a computer.

"Give me the gun, Nosey," he said.

Nosey handed it over cautiously.

"Now break all their longbows. We don't want—"

Someone started to run. Greville shot him in the back. "We don't want anybody popping off at us when we push off, do we?" he said imperturbably.

Two deaths in less than five minutes were quite sufficient to demoralise twenty men. They stared hypnotically at Greville as if he were holding a magic wand.

It took Nosey an incredibly long time to break twenty longbows.

"What next, mate?" he asked.

"Next," said Greville, "you use the string to tie these gentlemen's hands together."

That took even longer. One man grabbed Nosey while he was busying himself with the bow-strings and tried to use him as a shield. But Nosey had the good sense to drop to the ground, and Greville managed to shoot the offender through the shoulder. That left four bullets.

Greville looked back across the fields to the manor house, less than four hundred yards away. He thought that when they left, the hue and cry would be raised pretty quickly. Ahead, about the same distance from them, lay the line of trees that marked Brabyns Wood. The wood, he had learned from previous talks with Nosey, was about half a mile across. On the other side was more open country, and beyond that was the village of Lower Brabyns where the Squire's so-called anarchists lived.

Nosey, at least, had recovered from the shock and speed of events. "Everybody trussed something beautiful, mate," he reported with a grin. "We're doing a great job."

"Now," said Greville, eyeing the sullen line of men with their hands tied behind their backs, "now, we all play ring-a-roses and lie down."

Nobody moved. So another bullet crashed into the leg of the nearest man. He fell down. The rest lay down.

"Well?" said Nosey. "You've dropped us into the shit, proper, haven't you?"

For the first time Greville smiled. "I think it's about time we joined the annies," he said. "Are you any good at running?"

## TWENTY-SIX

When they heard the dogs behind them, Greville decided that he and Nosey would have a better chance if they separated. The dogs, presumably, had picked up the scent. Doubtless they would continue to follow only one scent; but even if they split up and followed both, the chances of individual survival were still surely better.

Nosey was not in very good shape. Neither, come to that, was Greville. He knew that he had set too hot a pace at the beginning. Altogether, they must have covered at least three miles by now. Brabyns Wood lay far behind them. That had been the easiest part of the flight. Since then they had been floundering through patches of half-frozen mud and the seemingly interminable and deceptive carpet of long dead grasses and weeds that covered what was once good farming land. Now they were shambling unsteadily up a long and gentle rise; and they could hear the excited barking of the dogs behind them. They were exhausted.

The village of Lower Brabyns could not be far ahead; but it was much farther from them than the dogs were. Greville turned and looked at Nosey's tortured face.

"Stop a minute!" The luxury of not having to push one leg in front of the other was so great that Greville didn't think he could start moving again.

"We've had it, mate," groaned Nosey. "We're outnumbered. Them fucking dogs has got four legs. We've only got two."

"So we separate," panted Greville. "Give them something to think about ... You go that way. I go this way ... Half a mile detour for each of us. Then we close on the village ... Here, take the gun."

Nosey still had some spirit left. "Keep it. You'll need it just as much as me."

"No time for arguing. Take the bloody gun. I'm tired of carrying it anyway ... And—good luck, Nosey."

Nosey took the gun and held out his other hand. "And the best of British luck to you, too, mate. We ain't going to make it, but what the hell." He managed a grin. "It was worth it just for Big Tom. So long."

"We'll make it," said Greville. "Get moving."

Greville sent a mental priority telegram to his legs. He stared down in amazement as one came out in front of the other. The movement developed into an unsteady walk. The walk broke into a tottering run. He didn't look back, which was perhaps fortunate. For Nosey did not move at all. He just sank gratefully down on the grass and stretched his aching limbs. Then he examined the revolver. Three bullets. Which left two for the dogs ...

Greville had covered more than three-quarters of a mile before he heard the shots. Mechanically he counted them. One ... A long pause ... Two ... A longer pause ... Three ..

Greville kept moving He was too tired even to think about Nosey. He knew that when he next stopped he would stop for good. So he kept moving. He had crested the hill and was coming down the far side. Consequently the dogs sounded a little farther away. He looked ahead, straining to catch a glimpse of Lower Brabyns. He thought he saw something that looked like a village in the distance; but odd patches of fog seemed to be obscuring his vision.

He wondered vaguely why the fog should be tinted with crimson, and why in the middle of the fog there should be strange little flashes of lightning. But he managed to keep moving. There was nothing else to do.

Presently he began to fall down. It was a frightening sensation because he seemed to be falling from a high building. It was frightening also because the temptation to lie where he had fallen was tremendous; and the energy required to pick himself up seemed to be more than mortal man could supply. Nevertheless, he did manage to pick himself up. Cursing at first, then groaning, then crying, then whimpering.

The world had become dark. He didn't know where he was going and he didn't even know where he had been. All he knew was that he had to keep moving.

Eventually there was no strength left to keep moving. He fell over something that seemed to cut into both legs. As he went down he thought he could hear bells ringing. Not church bells. Little bells. Oddly, he thought of James Elroy Flecker:

*When those long caravans that cross the plain*
*With dauntless feet and sound of silver bells*
*Put forth no more for glory or for gain,*
*Take no more solace from the palm-girt wells . . .*

And then he thought of palm-girt wells. And a hot sun pulsing energy out of an azure sky. He thought of sweaty camels and sweaty men with brown, lined faces. He thought of palm trees and water and music. And of the Samarkand that had existed only in a man's mind.

The vision was beautiful. Too beautiful to let go. But he was too tired to hold on to it. The sound of silver bells dissolved into silence. The sun was eclipsed. The oasis became dazzlingly black pools. And all that was left was night . . .

When Greville finally opened his eyes, he found that he was sitting in an easy chair. The first thing he saw was a log-fire spitting and crackling in an open hearth. The second thing he saw was a group of people—two men and a woman. The third thing he saw was a naked female torso. No arms. No legs. Only breasts like overripe melons and a belly that was so smoothly round that it surely contained all the fecundity of the cosmos. It was made of stone. Beyond the torso was another block of stone, roughly and vaguely carved, with two holes in it. Beyond that was a thing of iron. It might have been a twisted skeleton; it might have been a twisted bedstead; it might even have been a joke of a cage for an oddly mutated parrot. There was something about it that made Greville want to laugh.

He laughed.

One of the men spoke. "Well, well. Another bleeding philistine. Just my bleeding luck . . . Now that you've joined the party, brother, you'd better tell us who issued the invitation."

## TWENTY-SEVEN

HAVING told his story, Greville sank back in the easy chair, gazed hypnotically at the log fire and gratefully sipped the drink that had been given him—a very generous measure of good Scotch. Once he had begun to talk, he found—to his amazement—that it was difficult to stop. He had told them not only about Big Tom and Sir James Oldknow's military ambitions but about Liz and Francis, the cottage at Ambergreave and even about Pauline. He had talked for quite a long time, and at the end of it he was surprised to find that it all amounted to a public confession. At the end, he realised that he had simply been trying to justify himself—but for what and to whom he did not know. He felt empty and light-headed. The Scotch and the warmth of the room had eased the pain in his limbs and transmuted it into an almost delicious aching. He was curiously uncertain whether he was dreaming or had just awakened from a dream.

But at least he was alive ... I ache, therefore I exist ...

The three people regarded him intently. The two men—one weather-beaten and rock-like, the other tall and angular—were standing. The woman, full-figured, attractively faded and in her mid-forties, sat on the chair opposite Greville.

"We're not really anarchists, you know," she said. "That's just the Squire being two-dimensional. Actually, we're nothing but cranks, misfits and loafers. There's about a hundred and fifty of us; and we came together simply for security ... I'm Meg, by the way. The tall and rather intellectual-looking gentleman is Joseph. He fancies himself as a historian. The rugged individual is Paul. This is his studio. He's responsible for the sculpture that seemed to amuse you."

"We're an unholy trinity," remarked Paul drily. "Meg

lives with both of us. That's how we keep power in the family."

Joseph said: "They're just trying to confuse you. Actually, we're a sort of hereditary triumvirate. We were in at the beginning and so we got saddled with the decision-making. It works quite well, really. You see, there's only one basic commandment: try to do as little damage as possible. It amounts to a rather negative philosophy, I'm afraid, but the odd thing is it seems to work."

"Shit," observed Paul. "We've got a community that's holding its own simply because most people aren't too loopy to see where their own interests lie. We don't give a damn whether people are homosexual or Hungarian. We don't give a damn whether they are sex-crazed or schizophrenic. So long as they do their whack and don't bust up the furniture. We've got two prophets, one messiah and an eighteen-stone bitch of a spiritualist. We've got demented mechanics and phallic sculptors—that's me. We've got prostitutes—precious few of those, I'm afraid—and even bleeding saints, if there was anybody to canonize 'em. But they are all with it enough not to interfere with each other. Now, we picked you up more dead than alive on a telephone-wire Maginot Line devised by a black-hearted Negro called Alexander the Great. We're so damn crazy we'd think anybody normal—if there was anybody normal—was a hundred octane nuts. So are you in or out? If it's out, we'll give you a pack of food and boot you out of the village in the nicest possible way. If it's in, you don't say 'sir' to anyone, but you bloody well do what you're told until you find your feet. Now, what do you want?"

Greville liked Paul. He liked his aggressive honesty. He had a feeling that this was the kind of community in which he might possibly find a place. But before he could contemplate any kind of future, there was a problem to be solved.

"What the hell do you want?" demanded Paul.

Greville looked at him. "First of all, I want Liz."

Paul sighed. "How romantic! Sir James Oldknow has acquired her for breeding purposes. So what do you propose to do about it—go and ask him politely to send her down here, complete with trousseau and layette?"

"I thought you might help me."

"Did you now! And we're supposed to get ourselves chopped up just because you lost your woman? Think again."

Greville began to get angry. "If you sit on your backsides long enough, you'll find you've all been volunteered into the feudal system."

"I doubt it," said Meg. "Alexander, our little Negro friend, is so crazy he's worth two battalions. If Sir James Oldknow starts empire-building, he may live to regret it."

"Actually," said Joseph, "Sir James has already been kind enough to send us a deputation. They arrived about half an hour after you did. Sir James says he wants you back. He also says that though you've been rather naughty, he's prepared to forgive and forget. However, until you go back, Liz isn't going to get any more food ... Rather primitive, I thought, but doubtless quite effective."

"What are you going to do?" asked Greville.

"Nothing," said Meg calmly. "This isn't our problem. As Paul says, we don't propose to risk our people for someone we've never seen."

Greville was silent for a moment or two. "Can you give me any weapons?" he asked at length.

Paul laughed. "Sir Lancelot rides again! What the hell do you think you can do?"

"Not much," said Greville simply. "But I can try ... Will you give me any weapons?"

"We'll have to talk to Alexander," said Joseph. "He has acquired quite an armoury, so I expect something can be arranged." He gave Greville a thin smile. "I hope you don't know what you are doing ... Incidentally, and just to observe protocol, you'll have to steal whatever you need and leave us—in the best tradition—stealthily and by night."

Greville managed to raise a smile. "Oddly enough," he said, "that is exactly what I thought of doing."

## TWENTY-EIGHT

THE night was cold; but Greville had been given a couple of sweaters and a thick pair of corduroy trousers. There had even been two volunteers to go with him—hoping, doubtless, to acquire women of their own. But Paul had vetoed that idea. He had pointed out, somewhat drily, that if on the morrow any other bodies than Greville's were discovered, Sir James Oldknow would have a legitimate tailor-made reason for marching into battle. The one thing that was likely to bring unity to his mixed bag of followers was woman-stealing.

So Greville was entirely on his own. Alexander, the Negro, a pint-sized Napoleon who insisted on styling himself General of the Anarchists had been most kind. He had let Greville have an ancient but workable sten-gun, half a dozen magazines, two grenades, a knife and a suicide pill. Greville had not been particularly interested in the suicide pill, but Alexander had insisted. He claimed it was *de rigeur.*

As Greville made his way across the five miles of no-man's-land that lay between the two villages, he was thankful that the night was moonless and rather misty. He did not, however, harbour a great deal of optimism for his expedition. He knew that he needed more than darkness and the element of surprise. He needed about ten good men or about ten successive miracles.

He realised there was very little hope of being able to get anywhere near Liz. Probably Sir James had moved her out of the pen, anyway. But there was just a slender chance, thought Greville, that if he created enough diversions and raised enough hell he might get within shooting range of Sir James Oldknow himself. And even if he couldn't retrieve Liz, at least there was the possibility of scoring an eye for an eye . . .

Alexander himself had escorted Greville through what Paul had called his telephone-wire Maginot Line. It did indeed consist of stretched telephone wires. They had been threaded through empty tin cans and fixed at intervals to knee-high wooden posts. Between the wires small pits had been dug in the earth at random so that any force attempting a night-time invasion would make quite a lot of noise and probably collect a few sprained ankles in the process. It was on Alexander's Maginot Line that Greville had foundered that very morning.

Before Alexander turned back to the village, he gave Greville one final piece of advice. "Now, boy," he whispered, "remember there ain't no hurry in this thing. Take your time—you got all night. Move a little, then stop and listen like you was a goddam big microphone. When you find something moving, use the knife like I showed. And don't let the poor bastard have any chance to give you the playback. *Bon soir*, old chappie, *bon chance* and *bon* bloody *appetit*."

With muted chuckles, Alexander retreated into the darkness; and Greville was alone.

As the Negro had said, he had plenty of time—there were still two or three hours to go until midnight—but Greville was eager to get the whole thing over and done with. At least, he told himself grimly, when you are dead you no longer have to worry about being afraid or getting hurt.

So he pushed on through the winter night with a speed and lack of caution that would have made Alexander throw up his hands in despair. For a while, luck was with him, however. After half an hour and without incident he had reached Brabyns Wood.

He had also reached the end of his one-man assault upon the feudal system. For, as he soon discovered, Brabyns Wood was alive with men.

At first Greville thought they were Sir James Oldknow's private army, massing for a surprise attack upon the anarchists. But there were too many of them. And, by the light of several fires that had probably been used for warmth and cooking, he discovered an even more convincing reason why they could not be Sir James Oldknow's men. Each of them wore a monk's habit.

The sight was incongruous, fantastic, absurd—and terrible. Each of the "monks" carried a weapon of some kind. Several had rifles or shot-guns, but most were armed with spears or longbows.

At first Greville wondered why they advertised their presence so openly. But then, he reflected, there was no reason why they shouldn't. The Brothers of Iniquity were too numerous to be attacked by wandering bands of scroungers.

And that led to a torrent of questions. Why were they there? What did they intend to do? Which way did they intend to go? Would they turn south and obliterate the feudal system? Or would they travel north and devote their attentions to anarchism?

Greville's first impulse was to turn back and attempt to warn Alexander. But while he was doing that, the Brothers of Iniquity might well decide to tackle the nearer community of Upper Brabyns. The only thing to do, he decided, was to wait and find out.

He did not have to wait long.

As he crept cautiously nearer to Brabyns Wood, the fires began to be extinguished, one by one.

Then, to his immense surprise, he literally walked into one of the brothers—posted, presumably, as a sentry. Both men fell over. Even as he went down, Greville remembered Alexander's final piece of advice. The knife seemed to jump into his hand of its own volition. He struck once, and hit nothing but the earth. He struck again with the same result.

The man he had walked into evidently had better eyesight, for he managed to fling himself on top of Greville. But Greville still had the knife. Alexander had told him to aim either for the throat or below the rib cage and to strike upwards. But he didn't know where his assailant's throat was and he didn't know which way was upwards. He just plunged the knife in again and again, wherever the opportunity seemed to present itself. He expected screams, but there were no screams. And, uncontrollably, he kept on striking with the knife long after the man was dead.

Eventually, Greville rolled from under the body and picked himself up. No fires were visible now. There was nothing but utter blackness—and the sound of many men moving.

They were moving towards him. And that must mean that they had decided on Lower Brabyns.

Without thinking, Greville lay down once more by

the side of the man he had just killed. There was a warm wetness over his hands and face. Salty fluid trickled into his mouth. He didn't know whether it was his blood or the dead man's. He didn't care.

Columns of men passed on either side of him, not more than two or three yards away. He heard voices and occasional laughter. He waited until there was nothing more to hear at all.

Then he got up, and turned back in the wake of the Brothers of Iniquity. He was thinking of Francis and of the destruction that had been wrought at Ambergreave. He felt physically and spiritually numbed.

Theoretically, Alexander's Maginot Line would give warning of the attackers. But suppose it didn't? Suppose the Brothers of Iniquity had inspected it in daylight and were planning a detour? Or suppose that Alexander's sentries were not as alert as they should be? If this band of sadistic psychopaths got as far as the village they would soon make short work of anarchism and would leave behind them the same trail of desolation that they had left at Ambergreave.

Greville unslung his sten gun. He judged he was about fifty yards behind the rearguard. He judged also that in about ten minutes, unless the Brothers of Iniquity changed direction, they would be among the telephone wires and tin cans. That, no doubt, would be the time to signal the start of the party.

But the Brothers of Iniquity were nearer to Lower Brabyns than Greville had calculated. About two hundred yards ahead he heard what, less than twelve hours ago, he had interpreted as the sound of silver bells.

He quickened his pace. The need for silence was over. After about ten seconds he actually ran into one of the rearguard columns.

And then everything began to happen at once.

Greville emptied his first magazine into the darkness ahead. Screams and shouts told him that he had found targets. At the same time, a small searchlight was switched on somewhere in the village. It swept over the telephone wires, picking out the columns of advancing men.

Greville dropped to the ground, tore out the empty

magazine and slipped another one into the sten. Then he rose to one knee, firing at the same time, spraying the black lines that were negotiating the telephone wires to the sound of old tin cans.

Fifteen or twenty men fell as if they had been scythed. The rest evidently could not understand that the firing could be coming from behind them. With savage cries they forged ahead, eager to get to grips with the defenders.

Greville changed magazines once more and began to cut into another line of the advancing men. At the same time the Brothers themselves started shooting. And then there was a blinding flash, and another, and then an entire dazzling barrage of light.

Greville stood amid the Brothers of Iniquity, temporarily blinded. Arrows whistled. Rifles and light machine-guns began to chatter away. Bedlam reigned.

Suddenly, he felt a smashing blow in his shoulder. Then there was another one in his leg. He spun like a top, still firing the sten gun blindly. Then the whole hullabaloo seemed to be fading away. Overcome by a curious lethargy, he decided to sit down. The lethargy persisted. So he decided to lie down.

He didn't know it, but his finger was still crooked tightly round the trigger of the sten gun. He lay on his back, shooting blindly at the hidden stars until his magazine was empty.

The vibration stopped, and he knew that there was nothing left to worry about.

He had had a hard day, he thought dimly, and now it was time to go to sleep.

## TWENTY-NINE

GREVILLE opened his eyes. He was in a comfortable bed between clean, sweet-smelling sheets. He became fascinated by specks of dust dancing in a shaft of sunlight. Their movements were lazy and random—like tiny stars, he thought vaguely, dancing from nowhere to nowhere in a miniature cosmos.

He felt a dull pain that seemed to stretch down the left side of his body; but against the overwhelming fatigue that came down like a curtain, the pain didn't matter too much.

Beyond the shaft of sunlight, half-hidden by shadow, there was a woman's face. It looked a bit like Liz; but then it obviously wasn't Liz. The effect of concentration became too much for him.

"Hello," he mumbled thickly. "You're someone else, aren't you?"

Then he gave a great sigh and went back to sleep.

Six hours later, when the sunlight had given way to twilight, he woke up bathed in sweat and screaming: "Liz! Liz! Oh, Liz!"

Somebody lit an oil lamp; and there was Liz, standing by the bed, holding his hand, wiping the sweat from his forehead. He looked at her and could have sworn that she was real.

"See what happens when I'm not there to look after you," said Liz. "You made a fine bloody mess of yourself, didn't you?"

"I thought . . . I thought . . ." he babbled. "Goddammit, what's happened?"

"Not to worry. Everything's all right, love. Now go back to sleep. You'll live."

He tried to sit up, and the effort made him groan. Great knives of pain sawed away at the muscles of his shoulder. He collapsed sobbing.

"Here," said Liz, "drink this. They haven't got any pain-killers left."

Brandy slopped over his chin, but most of it found its way into his mouth. The burning sensation was utterly beautiful. The room got dark, and he found a nice warm whirlpool. The trick was to dive clean into the centre of it.

"Sleep," commanded Liz. "You've been pressing your luck. I'll be here when you wake up."

Once more he slept. And awoke before daylight. Thirsty but cool. The pain had gone away.

Liz was still there. The lamp was still burning.

"My love," said Greville. "Oh, my love!"

Liz smiled. "So you're still delirious, then?" She leaned over the bed and kissed him on the lips.

"Didn't you know bad pennies always turn up?" she whispered. "Now go back to sleep till morning."

"I want a drink."

"Brandy?"

"No, water."

Liz gave him a glass. "You must be someone else," she said happily. "The man I knew wouldn't have touched it."

Greville drank greedily, then closed his eyes.

Morning came. He opened his eyes, and Liz was still there. She lay curled up in a big chair, sleeping.

As the lamplight lost its battle with the increasing daylight, Greville studied her. Her nose was shining, her lips had fallen open. She was wearing a drab brown dress that fitted her like a potato sack.

Greville felt on top of the world.

He didn't say anything because he didn't want to waken her. If he had been a praying man, he would have said: "Thank you, Lord, for miracles gratefully received."

But he was not a praying man. He was simply glad to be alive, and glad that life included Liz once more. He looked at the swelling of her belly. Beneath the potato sack, beneath the flesh there was the absolute testament—a busy little colony of cells that would one day have the effrontery to call itself human.

What the hell did it matter who the father was? For he could only ever be the father in an empty biological sense. Whatever the stupid facts, no matter who provided the mechanics of the act, the child would belong to Greville and Liz. At the beginning, he thought half-cynically, it would be nothing more than a tiny blue-eyed computer. And he and Liz would jointly programme it. Perhaps they would make of it something that could look at the night sky and be moved to tears. Or perhaps it would turn into a twentieth-century Caligula. But whatever happened, it would belong to them alone. For they would make out of the clay a statue that would at least dance and take pleasure in the illusions of life . . .

He drifted into dreams again. It was quite late in the day when he next awoke. There were other people in the room besides Liz. Meg and Joseph.

"Congratulations," said Meg. "We didn't really have any doubts. Both bullets passed clean through. But congratulations. Another week or so, and you'll be bouncing around with the best of us."

"How the devil did you get hold of Liz?"

"We bought her," said Joseph. "It seemed the easiest way. After the Brothers of Iniquity had departed, we were in no position to take her by force—even if we had wanted to." He gave a tight smile. "However, our visitors themselves donated the price. It was, I recall, ten rifles and two hundred rounds of ammunition."

Greville was silent for a moment or two. "They'll use the rifles against you," he said at length. "Sooner or later, Sir James Oldknow will come charging down here with the Brigade of Guards and the Household Cavalry."

Joseph shrugged. "We hope it will be later rather than sooner. In order to teach him the facts of life, we invited him to see what had happened to the Brothers of Iniquity. The final count, I believe, was a hundred and fourteen dead. Of which, I may say, you appear to have accounted for at least thirty ... He was duly impressed."

"But not for long," observed Greville. "I doubt whether anything impresses the Squire quite so much as his own delusions of grandeur."

"Which is where you come in," said Meg. "Or where we hope you will come in. We lost about fifteen per cent of our strength, including Paul and Alexander. Since you are such an aggressive character, we rather hope that you might take up where dear little Alexander—rest his soul—left off."

Greville gave her a wan smile. "I'm not sure I'm community-minded enough for you people," he said. "I'm not even sure I have any faith in democracy."

Meg snorted. "Poof! Who wants democracy. You can't have democracy with a colony of nut-cases. What we need are benevolent despots."

"What he needs," said Liz pointedly, "is a bit of peace and quiet. Give him a chance to get some strength before you start filling his head with nonsense."

"You're quite right, my dear," said Joseph primly. He turned to Greville. "We'll come and see you again tomorrow. I'm rather afraid we need someone like you. But enough of that. I'll have some food sent up. Your bandages have already been changed, and I expect Liz can attend to your bodily needs . . . Anyway, thanks for helping us. You were the best investment we have made for a long time."

When Meg and Joseph had gone, Liz said impishly: "I like that bit about attending to your bodily needs. Have you got any?"

"Jump into bed and find out."

"Not today, thank you," she retorted. "I'm blowed if I'll have you passing out on me before I reach a climax."

Presently there was a timid knock at the door, and a child of about ten, a girl, brought in a tray on which there was a bottle of red wine, two glasses and two steaming plates.

"Venison and two veg," announced the child in awe. "Meg said you was to eat it all . . . But she said if there was any left over, I could have it.'

Greville regarded her benevolently. "I'm almost certain there's going to be quite a lot left over. Stay and find out."

The child sat at the foot of the bed and watched greedily while Liz and Greville ate. There was indeed a lot left over. Neither of them were very hungry. They were too excited at being together again.

By the time they had finished the meal, it was almost dark once more. Liz lit the oil lamp. Greville kept the bottle of wine and the glasses, and sent the child scuttling away with several large slices of venison.

"Chateau-neuf du Pape," he read the label on the bottle incredulously. "Where the hell did they get it?" He poured another glass for Liz and himself. "Had any good screws lately?" he asked casually.

"Dear love, as far as the Squire was concerned I was just a mare in foal. Three meals a day—until you became naughty—and nothing to do. The welfare state. I never had it so boring."

"Come into bed," said Greville, relaxing. "I can't do a bloody thing, but I just want you close."

"Amen," said Liz. She took off her dress and displayed the roundness of her belly. "You've got over it?"

"I've got over it."
She smiled. "I think I was crazier than usual ... It's going to be our child isn't it?"
"It's going to be our child," said Greville positively.
It was very difficult for them to touch each other without giving Greville a certain amount of pain; but after a time they learned the trick. Liz lay on his right side with their legs touching from hip to toe. To Greville it was like a benediction. He wanted to stay awake and savour the situation, but presently he was fast asleep.
When they woke up in the morning they were both stiff—Greville from his bullet wounds and Liz because she had hardly dared to move. They kissed each other in the grey, early light. They kissed each other and mumbled words that were nonsensical and profound, words that could have little meaning for anyone who overheard them, words whose only value was as the sound effects of pleasure ...
At length, Greville said: "I've been thinking."
"Why? I'm sure it's not good for you just now."
He patted her affectionately. "Because of that lump in your belly, I suppose ... We've got to live somewhere, haven't we?"
"Yes."
"We've got to have as much security as we can get."
"I suppose so."
"Then," said Greville, "we might as well join the Band of Hope—but only on our terms."
"Fine," said Liz equably. "What are our terms?"
"Ridiculous," said Greville. "Absolute dictatorship masquerading as sweetly reasonable co-operation ... They'll never wear it, of course. But at least I've got an ace to play ... Everybody is short of women. I think I know where I can lay my hands on about thirty."
"Where?" demanded Liz, wide-eyed. "Although," she added, thoughtfully, "I'm not sure that I want to know."
"The Convent of the Sacred Heart," said Greville. "Now you'd better make me presentable so that I can do a bit of hard bargaining with Meg and Joseph."
Meg and Joseph appeared shortly after breakfast. Liz was still in bed, naked; but neither of the visitors seemed disturbed or embarrassed.

"I trust you slept well?" said Joseph.

Greville glanced at Liz and smiled. "Adequately, bearing all things in mind."

"Have you thought about our proposition?" asked Meg.

"I have. And I'm going to make a little speech. After which, it's in your hands."

"Go ahead," invited Joseph. "Speeches are as yet unrationed."

"Well, mine goes like this. You people are trying to get together a community that works and will survive. As things are at present, you haven't got a chance. You survived the Brothers of Iniquity by the skin of your teeth. Your next problem is Sir James Oldknow with a fanfare of trumpets. And after him—if you survive again—there will be someone or something else. If it isn't people it will be dogs or rats or something like that. You're too exposed. You're too free and easy. And you're not growing. In fact, with every challenge that comes along, no matter what happens you can only continue losing ... Am I overstating the case?"

"Possibly," said Joseph, "but not so that one notices it. Proceed."

"Well, then, if you—or in fact anybody—wants to build a community that will last and expand you've got to go back to fundamentals. You've got to find a piece of land that's suitable and be prepared to hold it against all comers—human, animal or vegetable. Then you've got to get recruits. Then you've got to be able to expand as you need to expand ... You could try an island, of course—something like the Isle of Man or Guernsey or even the Isle of Wight. But all islands are at the same time too big and too small. They're too big when you start and too small when you really want to grow bigger. One thing is sure, you can't sit here in the middle of England indefinitely and hope it will all turn out for the best."

"So far," said Meg, "you've done nothing but state the problem. What about the solution?"

Greville's shoulder was beginning to throb, but he ignored it. "The solution is to find a piece of land which you can defend, on which you can expand and from which you can't retreat. Then you start recruiting.

And you don't recruit by inviting people to join you for tea and cakes. You recruit by taking the offensive against any nearby community that is either decadent—in the sense that it's going nowhere—or failing. In short, you steal people. You guarantee them food and a certain amount of freedom: in turn they give you a certain amount of 'co-operation'—no more, in both cases, than is strictly necessary. As time goes by, the amount of co-operation that's required will become less—we hope. As time goes by the amount of freedom that can be allowed will be more—we hope. But expanding will have to be the order of the day. That way you can grow. Any other way, and you've had it."

"That's all very well," said Joseph, wrinkling his nose, "if one wants to found a new society."

"What else is there to found?" demanded Greville calmly. "We've already got enough bloody chaos to last us for a thousand years. Liz has a child inside her. I'd like to think it's got some sort of bearable future. I'd like to think it's not going to have to spend the best part of its life just avoiding being killed by rats, cats, dogs or humans. I'd like to think it will get a chance to live."

Meg was getting exasperated. "Fine talk," she said icily. "You're still up in the air. Come down to earth and tell us what it's all about. Tell us what you'd like to do."

"I'd like you to give me absolute power for a year. Failing that I'd like you to leave me alone until I get well. Then Liz and I will push off after saying thank you very much."

"Absolute power," quoted Joseph, "'corrupts absolutely'."

"I'm corrupt already."

"To hell with that," snapped Meg. "What would you do?"

Greville smiled. "First of all, I'd get my strength back. Then I'd make arrangements to collect enough women to give us a decent chance of biological survival. Then I'd start a mass migration. I'd wait till the decent weather comes, then I'd take the whole community down to the tip of Cornwall. There might be somebody there already, of course. But in that case we'd either lick 'em or make 'em join us. If, on the other hand, they licked us, the problem would be solved anyway ... But if they didn't lick us, or if there was no one there in the first place, we could begin to build. We'd start with a couple of square miles of territory—backs to the sea and all that stuff. We'd clear it of all the livestock we didn't want and erect fences, barricades, ditches—anything to keep the rest out. Then as we grew we'd gobble up a bit more territory each year." He laughed. "A couple of generations from now, who knows, we might even get as far as Devon. Ten generations from now—providing we don't get another good dose of solar radiation— we would very likely get as far as holding a general election and filling the Houses of Parliament with people who couldn't do any real harm ... Now tell me I'm too far gone."

"You're far gone," said Meg. "But aren't we all ... You said something about collecting women, I believe. We need women very badly."

"Unless something drastic has happened," said Greville, "and we can't rule that out of course, there's a remarkable character called Father Jack who has about thirty women at the Convent of the Sacred Heart in Newmarket ... I think if we put the proposition to him in the right way, he might join us. But that we wouldn't know until and unless we sent someone to tell him all about the idea ... I think he'd join us if only because one man can't hope to survive a lot of bloody females for ever. He's quite a character, is Father Jack. He saved our lives once—on a purely commercial basis, of course."

Gerville felt exhausted. He was amazed at himself. He was amazed at the unfounded optimism, the glib talk, the unreasonable assumptions. He was amazed even that Meg and Joseph had heard him out. Most of all he was amazed that they did not laugh.

The scheme was hair-brained, impractical and doomed. It was nothing more than a sick man's fancy, a wish-fulfilment for a man so traumatised at the prospect of becoming a daddy that he was busy building new Jerusalems out of daydreams and a high temperature.

There was quite a long silence.

"It's mad enough to have a chance of working," muttered Joseph almost as if to himself.

"He's stupid enough and dangerous enough to make it work," said Meg grimly. She turned to Greville. "I suppose we'll have to make you emperor, as well."

Greville smiled. "No. I've just thought of a nice democratic safeguard. We'll have a monarchy but no king. I'll be simply the king's general ... If you ever get a king, he'll be able to sack me."

"Where did you say this convent of the whatnot was?"

"Newmarket."

"You think your Father Jack would agree?"

"If he doesn't, we could always beg, borrow or steal ... But he will."

"You know," said Meg thoughtfully, "I'm beginning to think that any direction is better than no direction ... How would you propose to open up negotiations with Father Jack?"

"I'd write him a letter."

"So all we need now," said Joseph drily, "is faith and a gentleman with a cleft stick ... You're a fool, Greville. An absolute fool. But then history was made by fools ... I'm very much afraid we're going to have to make you the king's general, after all."

Liz joined in the conversation for the first time. She threw back the bed-clothes and gazed at her stomach in amazement. "It's quickened," she exclaimed. "I feel as if I've just swallowed a squirrel with a big bushy tail."

## THIRTY

It was spring—a riotous and intoxicating spring that, coming after a fairly mild and wet February, had covered the land with a carpet of green and the trees with a thick powdering of buds almost a month earlier than it should have done.

Greville was riding with three other heavily armed men in a jeep along a weed-covered road where bumps and pot-holes were giving him considerable anxiety; for Liz, travelling with some of the women in a large truck about a hundred yards behind him, was in the last month of her pregnancy. The baby could arrive any time. But he did not want it to arrive on the road to Newmarket. The entire company—a hundred and twenty-three people—would rest up for a few days at the Convent of the Sacred Heart before they took the road once more to Cornwall. That would be the ideal time for Liz to have her baby. Then she could get a bit of strength back before they started on the last leg of the journey.

The jeep stopped, and the column of vehicles behind it stopped, as they had stopped once every half-mile or so all the way from Leicestershire. Presently the two motor-cycle outriders who had been forging ahead roared back into view and waved them on, signifying that the next half-mile of road was clear and navigable.

The jeep jerked forward once more and continued at the leisurely speed of fifteen miles an hour. The odd assortment of cars, vans, trucks and station wagons behind it dutifully kept the regulation convoy distance of fifty yards between each vehicle.

Looking back over the last few months, Greville was still surprised at the speed with which his ideas had been accepted by Meg and Joseph and the group of people they represented. He was even more surprised at the speed and ease with which he had assumed the role of "king's general". At first he had taken his office lightly, seeing it as no more than a temporary expedient for getting things done. At first the title itself had been no more than a joke, invented on the spur of the moment. But the joke had a hidden subtlety; and the title had stuck. It had amused everyone. It had provided a necessary focus for their sense of the absurd.

Only a monarch could depose the king's general. But there was no monarch. And if ever the group got tired of Greville's autocracy they would have to create a greater autocrat to bring it to an end. For the present, however, they were content. Greville had offered them something more than mere personal survival: he had offered purpose and direction. The odd thing was, he reflected, that even transies needed something in which to believe, some concept of a future that it was possible to build.

The joke, Greville realised, was on himself. He had never imagined that he really possessed qualities of leadership. He had never imagined that he could accept responsibility for the fate of an entire community. Yet here he was, a white-haired if rather juvenile Moses, leading a small tribe of crazy and credulous human beings to a promised Land's End.

Land's End . . . The finality of the title itself was symbolic. For if one was going to make a new beginning where better to start than at Land's End.

Greville moved his arm and felt a dull stab in his shoulder. The wound had healed beautifully; but there was always a stiffness when it was going to rain. He looked at the sky—clear blue with a few puffy white clouds. But he knew it was going to rain. The shoulder never lied.

The jeep stopped once more. One of the motor-cycle outriders, a boy of perhaps eighteen, roared back to it, pulled up with a flourish and a screech of brakes, and saluted Greville. "The convent is just over a mile ahead, sir." He grinned. "We made contact with their day-guard . . . Dead smashing!"

"Go back and tell Father Jack we'll be with him in ten minutes," said Greville. "Tell him not to worry about food or sleeping arrangements. All we'll need will be a bit of space."

"Yes, sir." The boy saluted again and slapped the butt of the rifle that was slung over his shoulder. Then he roared off again.

It was funny, thought Greville, how so many of the young ones had developed a sudden enthusiasm for military etiquette. They stood to attention at the drop of a hat. They saluted like mad. And they seemed to compete with each other in every possible way to obtain the favour of the king's general. He hoped it wasn't an omen. He had no intention of founding a military state.

Poor Joseph! Poor Meg! Nobody seemed to pay much attention to them these days. And how they hated the efficiency and discipline that Greville had imposed. Perhaps they saw him as an anachronism—a sort of fascist dinosaur that wouldn't lie down.

And yet whenever Greville talked with them in public, he made a great point of being deferential. He wanted everyone to know that the king's general existed only on sufferance. Oddly enough nobody seemed convinced. The prevailing attitude seemed to be that Meg and Joseph

—the remains of an ineffectual triumvirate—existed on sufferance, and it amused Greville to make them feel they were necessary as advisers.

The jeep was moving again. The road had given way to a narrow and overgrown track. The Convent of the Sacred Heart was only two or three hundred yards ahead.

Greville began to relax. The first part of the journey was over without a single casualty. It was, he felt, a major triumph. What was more important, Liz had not given birth en route. And that was an even greater triumph.

The jeep pulled up at the convent gates. Greville glanced round quickly. The jeep was covered, he was pleased to note, by two groups of Father Jack's young ladies, complete with rifles, sten-guns and machine pistols. Somewhere in the background he caught a glimpse of a bazooka team.

Father Jack himself, unchanged, still wearing the long black habit of a priest, came out through the convent gates and greeted him. "Forgive the welcome committee, but one doesn't take unnecessary chances ... I trust you had a reasonable journey, my son."

"Much better than I thought," said Greville. "Incidentally, how many girls have you got? My messengers said you had thirty-five?"

Father Jack sighed. "We were rather inconvenienced in January. A very bad month. The number is now twenty-seven ... How many men have you got?"

"Eighty-three."

"My, my," said Father Jack. "What lucky girls they are ... You realise, of course, that the whole expedition is ludicrous."

"Certainly. Life itself has become ludicrous. What have we got to lose?"

Father Jack smiled. "I don't know about you. But I personally have a great deal to lose—I'm happy to say ... I trust, my dear fellow, for the sake of your sanity, that you never have to be responsible for a body of women."

At that point, a small boy ran forward to the jeep. "Please, general," he said breathlessly, "it's Liz. I was told to say she had been taken short. They reckon the baby is going to come pretty soon. They said I was to tell you because you said you wanted to be there."

Father Jack beamed. "Well, well. An auspicious omen. Needless to say, we have our own maternity ward. Some of the girls are a trifle adventurous at times. Perhaps you had better bring your dear lady inside."

Greville's shoulder began to ache once more.

He looked at the sky.

It started to rain.

## EPILOGUE

JULY 7TH,—2011. Shortly after dawn.

A servant carrying a tray entered the tent of the Kaygee of the Army of the Western Republic. The servant coughed deferentially and set the tray down by the white-haired old man in the sleeping bag.

Greville was awake, but he pretended to be asleep. He thought the servant might decide to go away. He would have liked a few more minutes to savour his private thoughts.

But the man just stood there uncertainly, coughing and making discreet little noises, hoping to rouse his master without appearing to have actually done so.

Greville sighed. It wasn't the man's fault, of course. He had standing orders for the expedition: to deliver early morning tea every day fifteen minutes after dawn.

The man coughed again, louder. Greville sat up.

"Good morning, Kaygee. I hope you slept well."

"Well enough. What's the weather like?"

"It's going to be another fine day. A little early mist, but it will be gone by the time you have finished breakfast. Shall I pour, sir?"

"Yes."

Greville watched the level of hot, steaming tea rise in his cup. It was going to taste wonderful. It always did. He still had not accustomed himself to the luxury. It was only a year ago that some adventurous young captain had taken his windjammer as far as Ceylon and brought back the first cargo of tea for over thirty years.

As yet, thought Greville, sipping the delicious liquid gratefully, tea was only for the rich and the powerful. But soon other windjammers would follow the first; and then everyone in the Republic would be able to have his morning cup. Which would prove that God was in his heaven once more and all was right with the world.

"Another cup, Kaygee?" The servant held the pot expectantly.

"No thank you. That's quite enough."

The servant smiled, put the cup and saucer (fine bone china) back on the tray and went out of the tent. Greville amended his list of tea-drinkers to the rich and the powerful—and their servants. He knew that the pot would be drained and a pinch of carbonate of soda added to the tea-leaves to make them yield a second brew before they were thrown away.

He got out of the sleeping bag and stretched. Then he began to put on his clothes slowly, cautiously, methodically. At sixty-seven one did everything slowly, cautiously and methodically, he reflected. It was not an age at which one could easily afford sudden movements. Nor was it an age at which one could easily make lightning decisions . . . Or, having made them, understand why . . .

He stepped out of the tent, and sniffed the morning air. The sentry brought his rifle to the present and slapped its butt so hard that Greville winced. The man's hand must be tingling with pain, yet he stared ahead blankly.

"Way for the Kaygee!" he shouted ceremoniously, though there was no one in the immediate vicinity to obstruct the passage of the Kaygee.

"Good morning," said Greville.

"Morning—sir!" shouted the sentry, as if he were addressing a multitude.

"Dismiss."

The sentry slapped his rifle again and went ostentatiously through the ritual of dismissal.

Greville was alone. Except for the fact that if he so much as sneezed half a dozen men would appear from nowhere to protect the Kaygee against disaster.

He had marched a column of two hundred men all the way from Truro to London. And he still didn't know why.

There had been reasons, of course. There had to be reasons—otherwise Father Jack, the first President of the Republic, would not have given his official blessing. Greville would have come just the same; but for political purposes it was necessary for the Kaygee and the President to be in complete harmony.

The reasons he had given Father Jack were quite convincing: it was necessary—now that the Republic was thriving—to find out the state of the country, to explore the possibility of further recruitment, to look for various scientific and technical instruments that could not at present be manufactured by the Republic's resources, and to seek out any other organised communities with which the Republic might develop mutually profitable relations.

But Father Jack was not easily deluded.

"Greville, my son," he had said, "we have nearly seven thousand citizens, the economy is sound and I don't give a damn if the clever lads at Truro University need an electron microscope or whatever. As far as I can see, what they need first of all is a change of nappies ... But if you have set your heart on this expedition, then I'll have to give the official say-so, in which case it's just as well that you've got some nice official reasons. They don't mean anything to me but I suppose they'll keep the Council of Electors happy. Just don't get yourself killed, that's all."

And so, after a leisurely march across southern England, Greville's column was encamped in what had once been Battersea Park on the South Bank of the Thames. Today, they would enter what was left of the City of London. But that was not important to Greville. All that mattered at the moment was that he was about to keep a sentimental rendezvous.

It was almost eleven years since Liz had died. She had given him two sons and a daughter. Then all had been set for them to share a decade or two of contentment and relative peace. Except that she had developed cancer of the womb. When it got too bad, Greville himself had delivered the *coup de grace*. That was the way Liz had wanted it.

Two sons and a daughter. Conrad, twenty-nine, and —so they said—a brilliant biologist. But Greville was never really sure that Conrad was his own son; and, oddly, because of that he loved him more than the others. Then there was Jason, twenty-three, a born trouble-maker who thought that everybody who had ever lived had been crazy except, perhaps, Joe Stalin and Mao-tse-tung. And after Jason there was Jane, nineteen, and probably the most beautiful woman in the Republic. Jane was a born actress, as was evinced by the packed houses of Truro Theatre. She didn't look at all like Liz. She didn't look at all like Greville. Only Jason looked like Liz—which was, perhaps, why Greville couldn't carry out his duty and execute him when he had led the rebellion. About three hundred citizens had been killed before it was over. The death penalty was obvious and inevitable.

But, in the end, Father Jack had saved the day with his decree of lifelong exile. Jason had been packed off to Ireland to see if he could convert the savages to neo-Marxism.

Greville looked at the remains of Battersea Park in the early light. It was nothing more than a piece of wilderness—primeval, as if man had just set foot in it for the first time . . .

"Kaygee, will you breakfast now?"

Greville was snapped out of his reverie by the appearance of a bright young man with one star on his shoulder.

"I rather think I will not breakfast at all, thank you."

"But, Kaygee, the President himself instructed us to—"

"The President is over-anxious," said Greville. "Dismiss."

"Yes, sir."

"Wait a moment." Greville had a sudden thought. "The scouts have been across to the other side?"

"Yes, Kaygee."

"Did they establish any contact?"

"No, sir."

"Then we may take it that the bridge is clear and open?"

"Yes, sir."

"Good, I think I'll take a little walk. Give me two men and tell the Second that I'll be back in half an hour."

"But, Kaygee," protested the young man helplessly, "we have explicit instructions from the President not to let you—"

"Bugger the President," interrupted Greville calmly. "In the nicest possible way, of course. Now do what I said."

"Yes, Kaygee," said the young man miserably. "Will you confirm it in writing?"

"I'll confirm your arse if you don't move."

The lieutenant almost literally evaporated. He was replaced by two of Greville's bodyguard, armed with automatic rifles and grenades.

"Follow me at twenty paces, and don't let me know you're there unless it's a matter of life and death."

"Yes, Kaygee," they said simultaneously.

Pretending that he was entirely alone, Greville strode briskly forward, making his way out of the Battersea Park and towards the road that led to Chelsea Bridge.

I wonder, he thought, how many of them know what Kaygee stands for? Probably they think it's some mystical title that goes back to antiquity. A few of the older ones will know. But to the young ones, Kaygee is nothing more than an incantation. It's a word that means everything and nothing. It's not even something they can still make jokes about ... The trouble with people nowadays is that they take everything too seriously. Goddammit, there isn't a decent transie left!

He laughed aloud at the notion; and the men following him fingered their guns nervously. They had not heard the Kaygee laugh for a long time. They couldn't decide whether it augured well or badly.

The morning mist had already cleared. Greville stood on the grass and moss-covered roadway and gazed at Chelsea Bridge, twenty yards ahead. Then he turned to the two men who had been following him.

"You will stay here. I am going to take a short walk along the bridge. I'll be back in a few minutes."

"Sir. Permission to speak."

"Granted." There was a touch of annoyance in Greville's tone that boded ill for the man who had spoken.

"Sir, we are supposed to protect you," he continued desperately. "We cannot fulfil our duty if we have to remain here."

"You will not need to protect me on the bridge, and I shall not cross to the other side."

Greville turned away to avoid further argument. Really! They were treating him as if he were a baby. Something would have to be done about discipline. He could hardly move these days without stumbling over some well-meaning idiot armed to the teeth.

He walked slowly on to the bridge.

He looked over the side.

He was filled with childish delight.

The Thames was blue.

A blue river! He had seen plenty of blue rivers in the last twenty years. But somehow he had never expected that the Thames could turn blue once more. But having been free from industrial pollution for nearly forty years, what other colour could it be?

He was amazed and enchanted.

Greville turned his attention to the bridge. It was falling to pieces.

The suspension cables were coated with rust. So were the vertical wires. He doubted very much whether it would last another decade ...

A voice, familiar but unrecognised, came from nowhere and whispered in his ear: *"Love somebody ... Build something."*

Then suddenly the past came rushing back.

He remembered that night with Pauline. The cat that he had killed; and then the growing tension between them, resolved finally in the crash. He remembered Liz in the thin dawn light—a girl in a faded blue shirt and a pair of men's trousers that was two sizes too big for her. He remembered the dogs ...

But most of all he remembered two faces. Pauline's face, dead and beautiful: Liz's face, alive and innocent, pale and bruised.

It was all so long ago. So very long ago. Pauline belonged to another world; but Liz only belonged to another time.

And yet ... And yet they had both belonged to that other world.

So much had happened ...

So much that was strange and terrible. So much that was warm and intimate ...

Now, a new world was being born—a world in which the older people, the transies, were treated with a mixture of amusement and affection and fear; while the younger people, convinced of their own sanity and general soundness, were busy with dreams of new civilisations, new empires, new systems, new golden ages.

It was all, thought Greville, so sadly amusing. It was like Tchaikovsky's 1812 Overture—full of sound and fury, signifying nothing.

I am an old man, he thought. I have lived sixty-seven years and I am in my dotage. It appears that I have brought two hundred men all the way to London just so that I can keep a rendezvous with memories. I ought to be shot ...

When the bullet hit him, he thought it was the greatest joke of all time. He couldn't really believe it; but nevertheless it was very funny. He watched the blood make a mess of his nice clean uniform with amazement.

The first bullet slammed into his stomach.

The second bullet smashed his wrist.

The third bullet broke his leg.

He fell down.

There was a sound of automatic rifle fire as his two bodyguards rushed towards him, firing blindly across the bridge. They never reached him. For the enemy had automatic rifles also.

Greville was still conscious. He lay slumped by the metal parapet, staring at dents in the rusty ironwork. He felt a great surge of satisfaction. This was the very place.

He thought of Pauline. He thought of Liz. The two faces became blurred and indistinguishable.

*"Love somebody ... Build something,"* whispered that familiar but still unrecognised voice.

"I knew what it was to love," he said aloud. The thought surprised him. It also hurt him—more than the bullets had done.

"Goddammit I knew what it was to love!"

Things were happening at both ends of the bridge.

Greville's column had brought up their horse-drawn tank. The horses were released, and the tank roared forward under its own power and on the four gallons of precious diesel fuel that it still contained. Meanwhile, at the other end of the bridge, a bazooka came into operation. The first shot blew the turret off the tank, but it still continued on its way. The occupants were determined to get to their beloved Kaygee at all costs.

The second shot missed and hit one of the bridge suspension cables. It snapped like cotton. The bridge swayed and began to slant dangerously sideways. But the tank still came on.

Greville felt entirely happy. He had been hit by three bullets but he felt entirely happy. Or perhaps "satisfied" would be the better word. London was still alive.

"We've got a new civilisation going, Pauline," he babbled. "We're back to square one. Everybody wants to kill everybody else. It's quite exciting, really."

The second suspension cable snapped, and the bridge rested perilously on a single I beam. The tank came on: the bazooka continued firing.

Greville looked once more at Pauline's dead face. It dissolved. Then he saw Liz. "I'm sorry," she murmured, "I'm only good for screwing."

Greville reached out a hand to touch her. The pain was hitting him now and he found it hard to speak.

"I never really told you," he whispered with difficulty. "There weren't the words for it. You gave me much more than screwing. Much more even than love. You gave me—"

There was a great tearing. Th bridge sagged for a moment like crumpled cardboard. Then, taking Greville and the tank with it, it fell into the river.

The blue waters of the Thames foamed and clouded, turned grey, then dark brown. But presently they cleared as fragments of debris and a dead body, held up by a little air still trapped in its clothes, drifted slowly down the river, under the city's remaining bridges and out towards the sea.

It was a fine summer morning, promising a long warm day.